PENGUIN BOOKS

The
Gallipoli
Story

Patrick Carlyon was born in Melbourne in 1972.
He is a journalist with the *Bulletin*, and walked the
Gallipoli battlefields in 2000. This is his first book.

Patrick Carlyon

The
Gallipoli
Story

PENGUIN BOOKS

Penguin Books

Published by the Penguin Group
Penguin Books Australia
250 Camberwell Road
Camberwell, Victoria 3124, Australia
Penguin Books Ltd
80 Strand, London WC2R ORL, England
Penguin Putnam Inc.
375 Hudson Street, New York, New York 10014, USA
Penguin Books, a division of Pearson Canada
10 Alcorn Avenue, Toronto, Ontario, Canada, M4V 3B2
Penguin Books (N.Z.) Ltd
Cnr Rosedale and Airborne Roads, Albany, Auckland, New Zealand
Penguin Books (South Africa) (Pty) Ltd
24 Sturdee Avenue, Rosebank, Johannesburg 2196, South Africa
Penguin Books India (P) Ltd
11, Community Centre, Panchsheel Park, New Delhi, 110 017, India

First published by Penguin Books Australia, 2003

10 9 8 7 6 5 4 3 2 1

Cover design by Tony Palmer, Penguin Design Studio
Maps by Alan Laver, Shelley Communications
Front-cover photo of 7th Battalion troops courtesy of the
Australian War Memorial (F05577)
Typeset in Stone Serif by Post Pre-press Group, Brisbane, Queensland
Printed and bound in Australia by McPherson's Printing Group, Maryborough, Victoria

National Library of Australia
Cataloguing-in-Publication data:

Carlyon, Patrick.
The story of Gallipoli.

ISBN 0 14 300143 4.

1. World War, 1914–1918 – Campaigns – Turkey – Gallipoli
Peninsula – Juvenile literature. I. Title.

940.426

www.penguin.com.au

Contents

Author's Note **vii**

List of Maps

Conversion Table

Imperial measurements were used in 1915, as opposed to the metric system we all use today.

1 inch	2.54 centimetres		**1 centimetre**	0.394 inches
1 foot	30.5 centimetres		**1 metre**	3.28 feet
1 yard	0.914 metres		**1 metre**	1.09 yards
1 mile	1.61 kilometres		**1 kilometre**	0.621 miles

Author's Note

We learn the story of Gallipoli as we grow up. We hear about the dawn landing and the Australians who defied both the Turks and the elements to hang on to a miserable scrap of land on the other side of the world.

All the original Anzacs are dead now, yet the number of Australians who stand solemnly on Gallipoli's shores continues to swell each year. They come home and tell their friends and family how the visit moved them. And here is a simple truth – the story of Gallipoli thrives as one of our most compelling legends. Each year, it seems to grow stronger.

But there is more to Gallipoli than legend. There were brave Australians who landed there, but there were scared Australians, too. The Anzacs fought doggedly, but they made mistakes, too. They larked in the ocean and joked with their mates, but they also missed their families back home. Our first soldier volunteers looked for adventure; instead they stumbled into misery.

This book sets out to explore the events of Gallipoli in 1915. I have tried to find the facts, but it is not always possible to separate facts from legends. The more you know about Gallipoli, the more you will admire the men who fought there. Gallipoli may sound romantic to us, but it certainly was not for the men who fought, lived and died there.

Patrick Carlyon
Melbourne, 2003

EUROPE BEFORE THE GREAT WAR

CHAPTER ONE

A Black Coast

Pre-dawn, Sunday 25 April 1915

They huddled in lifeboats. Packs pinched their shoulders and their rifles felt heavier than usual. Legs stiffened and minds raced. What if a machine-gunner spotted them out here, sitting up like ducks on a pond? The soldiers had sharpened their bayonets the day before. A few bragged about how many Turks they would kill. The Turks would probably run away, someone said. No one believed that now.

They peered into the darkness and saw nothing. Just blackness. No one knew what lay ahead. Hell, they'd never heard of Gallipoli until a few weeks ago. A few weren't even sure how to spell it. Some smiled to show they weren't scared.

Some squeezed their eyes tightly and prayed that their legs would work. Just blackness. Why was it taking so long?

There were thirty-six lifeboats. Twelve steamboats towed them. There were thirty to forty soldiers in each lifeboat. These men would be the first of 12 000 Australians to land. Soon they would know that war wasn't as romantic as the people back home had said it was. The soldiers were farmers and lawyers, accountants and labourers. They had been the first to volunteer when war was declared in August 1914. They joined up thinking they were going to fight Germans in France. And here they were, bobbing on the Aegean Sea, wondering if Turkish snipers could see them through the mist.

The landing was supposed to be a surprise. But the Turks had to know now, didn't they? Surely they could hear the steamboats chugging? Shall we been seen, or not? thought Sergeant W. E. Turnley, a telephone mechanic from Sydney. Why don't the -------- fire at us?

The first lifeboats neared the shore. The steamboats released their tows. Oars plopped in the still water. A hill jutted above the shore. It was like a black fist warning invaders to stay away. Were there Turks in the shadows below?

A flame suddenly crackled from the funnel of one of the steamboats. It rose a metre and flared for twenty seconds or more. The engine had gone amiss. At once a yellow light gleamed high in the hills to the south. Now the Turks knew.

The boats were about to nudge into the wrong beach.

They had bunched up in front of Ari Burnu, a steep rise tumbling to the sea. Perhaps the tides had pushed the boats together. More likely, the warships that had brought the troops to within a few kilometres of the shore had anchored too far north. Not that it mattered now. In the smudgy light before dawn, the soldiers gazed up at soaring cliffs. They were supposed to be looking at a pleasant beach with a low hill behind it.

'Tell the colonel that the damn fools have taken us a mile too far north,' the naval commander yelled in the darkness.

'Look at that,' shouted Captain Ray Leane.

A man stood on a hill ahead. There was a shout from the shore. A single shot rang out. A bullet hissed over the Australians' heads. Silence. More shots. More hisses. The Gallipoli campaign had begun.

4.29 am

Queenslanders were the first to leap into the water and slip on the pebbly seafloor. Lance Corporal George Mitchell, of South Australia, was about 100 metres from shore. He saw a line of rifle-flashes near the crest of Ari Burnu. 'Klock-klock-klock, wee-wee-wee came the little messengers of death,' Mitchell later said. 'Then it opened out in a terrific chorus . . . The key was being turned in the lock of the lid of hell.'

Men crouched low in the boats to avoid the bullets. Here

and there they crumpled 'with a sharp moan or low gurgling cry'. They had been told the bullets would sound like small birds flying overhead. A cheeky private looked up and said to his mate: 'Just like little birds, ain't they, Snow?'

Captain Eric Tulloch would be wounded later in the day. The brewer would see out four years of war only to be killed by a burglar in his Melbourne home. For now, he just wanted to reach the shore. The boat on his left was drifting. The men on board appeared to be slouching. They had been hit by Turkish fire.

Lieutenant Ivor Margetts was a young teacher from a private school in Hobart. He was 193 centimetres tall and a keen Aussie Rules footballer. He landed a few minutes after the first wave. His battalion had piled into their first tow 'amid a perfect hail of bullets, shrapnel and the rattle of machine-gun'. He was ordering men into the second tow when the soldier in front of him fell to the deck, shot in the head. Others were hit as they were rowed to shore.

'Get out,' Margetts yelled, as his boat crunched on the shingle. His men jumped over the sides, arms above their heads to keep their rifles dry. All along the beach dozens of men splashed in the water. The heavy packs pulled them under. Mates tried to haul men up but some drowned. Margetts slipped twice before getting his footing.

He staggered onto the sand. Bullets struck sparks at the men's feet. Shrapnel shells exploded like puffs of cotton wool above. Turkish fire screeched and boomed and rattled. Margetts was luckier than some. Four boats, carrying 140 men of the 7th Battalion, came under machine-gun fire. More than one hundred men would be dead or wounded when the boats reached the shallows.

Perhaps Donald and Arthur Veitch were among them. They enlisted in Fitzroy, Melbourne, on 17 August 1914. Arthur was only sixteen years old but he told the recruitment officers that he was nineteen. Donald was in his early forties but said he was younger. They sat in the same lifeboat. They probably died side by side in the boat or as they clambered ashore. Back home, Mary Veitch would grieve the loss of her husband and son and wonder how she would raise eleven children on her own.

Margetts and his men took cover under a ridge and wriggled out of their packs. Wet sand clogged their unloaded rifles. Margetts peered up. How would he get to the top? To his right, men were already pushing through the prickly bush on Ari Burnu. They clutched at roots to haul themselves up.

Margetts dragged himself up a tawny slope that was even steeper than Ari Burnu. He came upon a trench but the Turks had already retreated to the tangle of gullies and ravines ahead. They shot back at the Australians, their bullets humming like bees. Margetts found his commanding officer, Colonel L. F. Clarke, a 57-year-old shipping manager.

Clarke was panting from his climb. It wasn't his fault he

didn't know where he was. His troops were scattered across hundreds of metres. So much for his orders. They'd said he was to form up and wait in reserve. Clarke was scribbling a message to headquarters – wherever that was – when he was shot in the heart. He died with a notebook in one hand and a pencil in the other.

Some soldiers remembered their orders and raced ahead. Others wandered about searching for their commanders.

It wasn't meant to be like this.

Major Walter McNicoll, a teacher from Geelong, had fretted over his 6th Battalion troops as they climbed into the lifeboats, silent and scared. 'Then began the strain of waiting,' he wrote later.

How would we face it? The question was never spoken aloud, but each man asked it of himself, and wondered if his neighbours were doing so too. They were trained to the minute . . . their minds prepared to guide those bodies rightly to meet any and every emergency. But in all this training the big element of 'the man who hits back' had been absent . . . The bayonet would no longer be thrust viciously into an inoffensive and spineless sack. Our future targets would not wait patiently for the marker to flag the result. How would we face it?

CHAPTER TWO

The Rush to Enlist

Joe Cumberland was said to be the youngest train driver in New South Wales. He was a friendly soul, tall with blue eyes, and one of the first to enlist from the Hunter Valley when England declared war on Germany. Cumberland did not need to know how the Great War, as it would be later called, began. Few Australians did. They simply knew that Germans had invaded Belgium. Cumberland was unquestioningly loyal to the British Empire. If Britain went to war, so did Australia. No need to think about it.

Europe had lurched towards war after a Serbian terrorist shot dead an Austrian archduke in Sarajevo, the capital of Bosnia, on 28 June 1914. We now know this as 'the shot that echoed around the world'. Austria had annexed Bosnia several years earlier, which antagonised the Serbs. But there is no evidence that the terrorist was acting for the Serbian government. Austria pretended that he was – it had wanted to invade Serbia for years. Now Austria placed impossible demands on its neighbour.

Russia backed Serbia. Germany backed Austria. By late July 1914, Europe had divided into two armed camps. On one side were Germany and the Austro–Hungarian Empire, on the other, France and Russia. Britain tried to find a diplomatic solution, but Austria kept threatening Serbia and on 28 July, declared war. Now the alliances came into play. Russia went to war against Austria. Germany invaded France, through Belgium. Britain, bound by treaty to defend Belgium, declared war on Germany. This automatically brought Australia and New Zealand into the war.

Few in August 1914 thought the conflict would last long. Many thought the war would be over by Christmas. Some nations, including Turkey, waited. They wanted to see who might win before they made a commitment. Unlike World War Two, the Great War wasn't about a clash of beliefs. There was no creed, such as Nazism, to be challenged. There was no madman, such as Adolf Hitler, loose in Europe.

The Great War grew out of jealousies and fears and misunderstandings that had been simmering for decades. Germany wanted to expand its borders. Austria wanted to extend its influence in Serbia and the Balkans. Russia also eyed the Balkans – and the Turkish capital, Constantinople. None of these nations had any idea that they would create a conflict that would leave 21 million people dead.

Cumberland celebrated his twenty-first birthday on board a troopship sailing to Egypt. His brother Oliver, twenty-five years old, had rushed from his job on a Queensland cattle station to be with him. Oliver wanted to protect his brother. Their sister Una fretted over them. She wore a purple and green brooch – the 2nd Battalion colours – as a good luck charm. The brothers sent her letters asking that she take good care of their little sister Dorrie.

'I got in by the skin of my teeth,' Oliver wrote to Una the day before they sailed.

> But I know Una that in your heart you won't blame me.
> I could not see Joe go alone and remain behind myself
> and I think it will be better now that we are together. I
> promise you I will never leave Joe wounded on the field
> whilst I have the strength to carry him off, and I know he
> will do the same for me.

Australian men rushed to enlist. Some 30 000 Australians and New Zealanders sailed in the first convoy, which left for Europe less than three months after war was declared on 4 August 1914. By the end of that year, almost 53 000 men had joined up across Australia. Many were more scared of missing out on the war than fighting in it. Most thought the British Empire would destroy the Huns, as the Germans were called, within six months.

People lined the streets to cheer the volunteers parading through capital cities. Thousands of Union Jacks fluttered among the crowd at Parliament House in Melbourne. Volunteers received civic send-offs in country towns. It was as if Australia had been waiting for the opportunity to present itself on the world stage. 'It is our baptism of fire,' declared the *Sydney Morning Herald*.

Enlistment Figures During 1914

	Aug	Sept	Oct	Nov	Dec
NSW	Total of 20 761				
VIC	6326	2929	2512	1366	1714
QLD	1481	1556	1386	673	1054
WA	Total of 4096				
SA	2012	921	493	658	728
TAS	981	487	167	163	97

Crowds waited outside the *Age* office in Melbourne for the latest war news. They broke into renditions of 'Rule Britannia' and 'Soldiers Of The King'. Faith in the British Empire was blind. Strange as it seems now, most Australians thought the British race the most superior on earth. In the

1911 census, 96 per cent of the population of 4.8 million considered themselves British, even if their families had lived in Australia for generations.

Both candidates for Prime Minister at the 1914 federal election, Joseph Cook and Andrew Fisher, were born in Britain and had worked in coalmines as children. Neither man disputed that Australia should put 20 000 Australian men at the British government's disposal. Campaigning in a Victorian country town, Fisher declared that Australia would defend the motherland 'to our last man and our last shilling'.

'Hundreds of thousands of Australians had unconsciously been waiting even before the war for such an event,' writes historian Geoffrey Blainey. 'Without knowing what event was needed they longed for Australia to parade in triumph before the nations of Europe. Here at last, they decided, was that triumph.'

Australia had much to learn about war. When death rates later soared and enlistment numbers sagged, the Australian government tried to conscript men. But the public wouldn't have it. By 1918, nearly 65 per cent of the 332 000 Australian men who had joined up had been killed or wounded. Nearly 60 000 were dead.

No one could have predicted this in 1914. Few spoke out against the war. Germans living in Australia were spat upon and locked up. The St Kilda Football Club, in Melbourne, changed its colours when it was noticed they matched those of the German flag. As one writer has noted, Australia

> didn't know what it was like to lose the best spirits of a generation, to read casualty lists that took up whole columns in the newspapers, to see young men return home old and broken and wanting nothing much to do with anyone for the rest of their lives.

Spy-mania

As Australia prepared for war, the civilian population was asked to report suspicious behaviour. Spy-mania swept the country. A report of lights flashing Morse code messages from the Dandenongs in Melbourne turned out to be nothing more than a rabbit-trapper carrying a hurricane lamp. Residents in New South Wales mistook a meteorite for an airship. Whales playing in the bay of a seaside resort were reported as an invasion of German submarines.

Men began enlisting in Melbourne on 5 August. Australia's most senior army officer, Major General William Throsby Bridges, insisted that the Australians fight as a single force. Had he not, Australian troops would have been shared out among British forces. There would have been no Anzacs and no Gallipoli legends.

Australia's official historian of the Great War, Charles Bean, described the first men to enlist as the most 'romantic' and 'adventurous flotsam that had eddied on the surface of the Australian people'. Those rejected at one place would try at another. One man rode his horse 720 kilometres to Adelaide, to be told there were no vacancies. He sailed to Hobart, and finally managed to enlist in Sydney.

The entry requirements were meant to be tough. Men had to be aged between nineteen and thirty-nine, though many sixteen-, seventeen- and eighteen-year-olds lied about their age. Recruits had to be at least 167 centimetres (5 feet 6 inches) tall. They had to have a good set of teeth. Men with flat feet or signs of corporal punishment were turned away, as were women doctors who offered their services. Camps were set up in Sydney and Melbourne before tents were found for men to sleep in. Privates were paid six shillings a day, about the equivalent of the average wage.

Men of Aboriginal appearance were rejected at first but later some were recruited to fight for the Empire. It's difficult to know how many Indigenous people served in the Great War, because accurate records were not kept, but estimates range from 300 to 500 men.

The recruits wore khaki woollen jackets with four big pockets. The buttons were dulled so that they did not glare in the sunlight. They also wore slouch hats with the badge of the rising sun, webbing belts and packs, and brown boots. About half of the first division of 12 000 men enlisted straight from their everyday jobs. Nine in ten soldiers were unmarried. One in five was aged twenty-one or under.

David McGarvie, twenty-two, of south-west Victoria, was told to go home when he tried to enlist in Camperdown. McGarvie was a crack shot and rode horses well, but the doctor laughed at him. McGarvie had a cleft palate and a muffled voice. Kids had teased him at school. A few weeks later he tried again in another town. He was accepted.

In Western Australia, a drifter from northern England enlisted as a stretcher-bearer. John Simpson Kirkpatrick smuggled a small possum onto the ship and let the animal run around inside his shirt. He thought he was getting a free ticket home to see his mother and sister. In life, he was just another battler. In death, he would become a folk hero.

The first convoy of 38 ships transporting troops to the European conflict left Albany, in Western Australia, on 1 November 1914. Life on board the convoy was dull, except when the *Sydney* shot up the German light-cruiser *Emden*, eight days out of Australia. Everyone celebrated with a half-day holiday. There were regular boxing matches and concerts. Each soldier was issued with an identity disc to put around his neck. Some Australians held the disc to their eye, to mimic

British officers who wore monocles – 'Haw haw,' they would joke.

Few on board any of the ships knew that Britain had declared war on Turkey. It wouldn't have mattered if they had known. They were sure they were going to fight Germans.

YOUNG OFFICER: "HAW, HAW, NO SHAVE?"
AUSTRALIAN: "HE, HE, NO – RAZAW!"

AN ILLUSTRATED PAGE FROM *THE ANZAC BOOK*, PRODUCED BY ANZAC
SOLDIERS IN GALLIPOLI, 1916.

CHAPTER THREE

War Games

November 1914 – March 1915

The Australians were dropped off in Egypt for more training. They lived in tents at Mena, near Cairo, and quickly became bored with desert drills and long marches. The soldiers awoke to a bugle and trained in the shadows of the pyramids. They cut their long trousers short because of the heat, and laughed because they looked like schoolboys. Some were disappointed they had not sailed to England. John Simpson Kirkpatrick, for one, expected they still would.

Cairo was a new world. Sand got 'in your tucker, in your ears, eyes, nose, everywhere and anywhere'. Arab hawkers bugged the soldiers to buy oranges or souvenirs. The

Australians learned new words such as *imshee yalla* (go away) and *igri* (hurry up). 'They are the funniest people on earth,' Joe Cumberland wrote to his sister. 'They all dress in gowns like you see in pictures in the bible.'

Egyptian Escapades

The Australian troops in Egypt had to be back in camp by 9.30 pm every night. From 9 pm most nights, the road from Cairo took on the appearance of a modern-day traffic jam. Phillip Schuler, war correspondent for the *Age*, described the 'whooping Australians' urging their donkeys on as cars and trucks sped past. 'By great good fortune no disaster occurred: minor accidents were regarded as part and parcel of the revels', Schuler wrote.

Many Australians climbed the pyramids. Walter Cass, Brigade Major to the 2nd Brigade, in a letter to his future wife, dated 16 November 1914, wrote of two climbers: 'Hundreds of our fellows have gone up – two never will again for one slipped and fell from about 2/3 of the way up. He broke most of the bones he has – his skull included – but is still alive. The other tried to climb the second pyramid by himself at night. He was found next morning but is done for all time. The doctors have lifted the pressure from the spinal cord but he will be paralysed for all time so they say.'

The Australians gained a reputation for unruliness. A joke went around about a sentry confronting men returning to camp at night:

Sentry: Halt! Who goes there?

Voice: Ceylon Planters' Rifles.

Sentry: Pass, friend.

(*later*)

Sentry: Halt! Who goes there?

Voice: Auckland Mounted Rifles.

Sentry: Pass, friend.

(*later*)

Sentry: Halt! Who goes there?

Voice: What the ---- has it got to do with you?

Sentry: Pass, Australian.

Some Australians went into Cairo, got drunk, and brawled. Christmas Day 1914 was especially bad. 'The Australians are notorious characters when let loose and on this occasion they completely ran amuck,' said a 3rd Battalion sergeant. A British general accused the Australians of blowing their wages on 'rather naughty' pursuits. Maybe he was right. Hundreds caught sexually transmitted diseases from local women. They had their pay docked. In February 1915, 120 men copped the cruellest penalty of all. They were sent home.

The Australians were now known as the Australian and New Zealand Army Corps. Clerks stamped A&NZAC on official papers. That's how the word 'Anzac' began.

Who's Who of Gallipoli

Herbert Asquith British Prime Minister

Lieutenant General William Birdwood Commander of the Australian and New Zealand Army Corps

Major General William Bridges Commander of 1st Australian Division

Winston Churchill First Lord of the Admiralty

Joseph Cook Australian Prime Minister till 17 September 1914

Andrew Fisher Australian Prime Minister from 17 September 1914 to 27 October 1915

Major General Alexander Godley Commander of Australian and New Zealand Division

General Sir Ian Hamilton Commander-in-chief of the Gallipoli groundforce

William Hughes Australian Prime Minister from 27 October 1915

Major General Aylmer Hunter-Weston Commander of British 29th Division

Lieutenant Colonel Mustafa Kemal Commander of Turkish 19th Division, and later commanded troops at Suvla and on the north flank of Anzac

Field Marshal Lord Herbert Kitchener British Secretary of State for War

Colonel William Malone Commander of New Zealand Wellington Battalion

Colonel John Monash Commander of Australian 4th Brigade

General Otto Liman von Sanders German Commander of Fifth Turkish Army

Lieutenant General Harold Walker Commander of 1st Division, after Bridges

The men heard rumours about where they might be sent. They didn't know of the political intrigues in London. In offices scented with leather and cigars, Britain's most powerful men tinkered with a bold scheme to 'knock Turkey out of the war'.

12 March 1915

General Sir Ian Hamilton had been a soldier for forty-two years when Lord Kitchener, the British Secretary of State for War, summoned him for a brief chat. Hamilton was a brave man, twice recommended for the highest honour, the Victoria Cross. He limped from a horse-riding fall and a bullet wound in the Boer War had crippled his left hand.

Hamilton was sixty-two years old and not at all like the British generals who commanded troops in France. He was tough but not ruthless. He was kindly and courteous and didn't like confrontations. He liked to write and did so with style. Hamilton had the temperament of an artist rather than a general.

Kitchener, a stern man with mad eyes, ordered Hamilton to lead a British army attack on Turkey. British warships already lay anchored outside the Dardanelles, the narrow straits that joined the Sea of Marmara, and the Black Sea beyond, to the Aegean Sea. Half of Russia's exports sailed through the Dardanelles. Turkey wasn't considered all that important in 1914. Except for its control of the Dardanelles.

Kitchener told Hamilton that British ships would steam up the straits and knock out the ancient forts lining the waterway. The ships had to sail about 21 kilometres up the Dardanelles before they would pass through the Turkish defences. The prize, several hundred kilometres further on, was the majestic city of Constantinople. Hamilton's forces would land only if the warships failed. Kitchener thought this very unlikely. One glimpse of a Union Jack, he said, and the Turks would run.

Hamilton knew little of Turkey, its soldiers or the terrain. He didn't even know how many men he was to have. As Hamilton later recounted in his memoirs, Kitchener resumed writing at his desk. He expected Hamilton to bow and leave the room. Kitchener was imperious and short-tempered. Querying him required a measure of courage. But Hamilton needed at least a few details. 'I must ask you some questions,' he said tentatively.

Kitchener impatiently explained that Hamilton would have about 70 000 men, including 30 000 from Australia and New Zealand. Some of the British troops would be on 'loan' from France only until the job was done. When Hamilton's chief-of-staff asked for planes and pilots, Kitchener's 'spectacles flashed'. 'Not one,' he said. After all, Turkey was only a sideshow. Kitchener's big war was in France and Belgium.

Hamilton left for the Dardanelles the next day. He read what information he had – some notes, an old Turkish army textbook and two small guidebooks. Kitchener wasn't the only British leader to think that the Turks would shrivel at the sight of British battleships.

Britain lost the race to win Turkish support at the outset of the war. British and German diplomats had courted Turkey – or the Ottoman Empire, as it was then known. They negotiated with the leaders of the Committee of Union and Progress, the Young Turks. In 1908 the Young Turks had overthrown the sultan.

The empire once stretched from Hungary to the Sahara, but it had been crumbling for centuries, weakened by corruption and conflicting cultures. Now it was bankrupt. Had been for more than forty years. The Young Turks acted like a society of gangsters. They got rich while some of their soldiers went barefoot. With Russia as its traditional enemy, Turkey needed help. Its leaders put the country up for auction. The Young Turks didn't believe in either side's cause. They simply wanted to stay in power.

German diplomats offered a German–Turkey pact against Russia. Britain then made Turkey's decision simple. Two Turkish warships were being built in Britain at a cost of £7.5 million. Turkey had raised the money through public subscriptions. Women had sold their hair to drop coins into collection boxes. On 3 August 1914, Britain confiscated the ships and offered no refund. The Turks were greatly offended.

Germany offered the Turks two battleships to replace the British ones. When these German ships arrived in Constantinople, the German sailors donned the Turkish Muslim headwear, the fez, as a sign of goodwill. German seamen headed up a Turkish fleet that attacked Russia from the Black Sea. The Young Turks closed the Dardanelles. One of Russia's most crucial trading routes was blocked. Russia declared war on Turkey. Britain followed later.

A young British politician, Winston Churchill, the First Lord of the Admiralty, wanted to force the Dardanelles. Today, he is best remembered as the prime minister who inspired Britain in World War Two. In 1915 he bamboozled political opponents with his deft mind and fine words. The Dardanelles scheme had tantalised him for months. He had already ordered the troopships carrying Australian and New Zealand troops to stay in Egypt, rather than sailing on to England as planned.

Churchill's colleagues on the War Council had wearied of long casualty lists from the Western Front. Why don't we outflank the Germans? Churchill argued. Why don't we invade Turkey? A few British ships would scare the devil out of them. And if Britain lost a few old ships, what would it matter? Churchill won tentative approval for his plan in January 1915, despite much argument.

In November 1914, the British had bombarded the outer forts of the Dardanelles and killed eighty-six Turks. In response, the Turks had laid mines across the strait, reinforced the forts, and brought in mobile guns. They waited for the British naval assault. They expected to lose. Constantinople was in a panic. The Young Turks began planning to blow up grand buildings, such as the Sancta Sophia church, so that the British could not have them.

How could Britain be stopped? The Turkish guns were old, ammunition was short, and the British navy had won victory after victory for the past 200 years.

Churchill fiddled with his scheme. No one except him fully understood it, mainly because it kept changing. Was Britain committing to a half-baked raid or a full-blown invasion?

Some British leaders thought troops should be landed, others not. Navy commanders worried about what their minister was proposing. The Secretary to the War Council, Lieutenant Colonel Maurice Hankey, expressed his doubts to the prime minister, Herbert Asquith. 'All through our history such attacks have failed when the preparations have been inadequate, and the successes are in nearly every case due to the most careful preparations beforehand,' he wrote. No one took much notice of him.

18 March 1915

Britain launched its naval attack. The sun shone as three lines of British and French battleships sailed into the Dardanelles.

The earth shuddered as forts disappeared behind clouds of smoke. Great fountains of water erupted around the ships as the Turks fired back. By early afternoon, most of the Turkish guns had stopped firing.

No one expected what happened next. A French ship, the *Bouvet*, suddenly growled and keeled over, billowing smoke. She sank in less than three minutes and 639 sailors drowned. A British ship, the *Inflexible*, lurched to starboard near the same patch of water. Soon after, the *Irresistible* listed and drifted towards shore. Then the *Ocean*'s steering gear jammed so that she went around in circles.

The British were shocked. Three ships sunk and another three badly damaged. Eleven days earlier, a Turkish captain, Hakki Bey, had watched the British ships on sorties near the mouth of the strait. He noticed that they all turned around at the same place. Bey laid a line of mines parallel to the shore at that place. His mines blew up the *Bouvet*, *Irresistible* and *Ocean*. The humble captain changed the course of the war in Turkey. Had it not been for these mines, Australians might not have landed at Gallipoli.

One of the Young Turks was so convinced that Constantinople would fall that he had two cars loaded for a quick escape. It is said that on the morning of 19 March, the Turkish gunners had only thirty shells left for their big guns. The British would probably have broken through, if they had tried. But the naval commanders weren't used to losing ships.

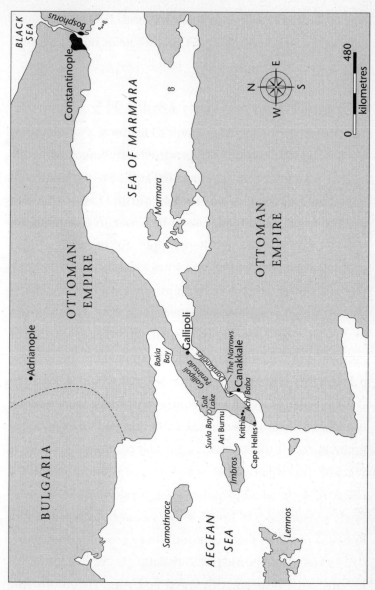

THE GALLIPOLI THEATRE OF OPERATIONS

They conjured excuses not to attack again. Hamilton agreed to land his men. He just wasn't sure where or how.

February, March and early April, 1915

The Australians sailed from Egypt to Lemnos, a Greek island off the Turkish coast. They practised climbing down rope ladders with full packs. They scoffed at the French soldiers in their blue jackets and red trousers. Gossip had it that any landing force at Gallipoli would lose four in five men. Yet some Australians were disappointed to be there – Turks couldn't fight like 'white' men.

The British army bought ships, mules, horses and water tanks from all around the Mediterranean. The operation was in disarray. The navy refused to attack the Dardanelles at the same time as the landing. Supplies got mixed up. Troops were delayed. No one knew how many Turks would defend the Gallipoli peninsula. Or how much fresh water there was. Or how best to treat the wounded. Hamilton had an even bigger problem. The Turks knew his army was coming.

The Turks had gathered 60 000 troops and appointed a German, General Otto Liman von Sanders, to lead them. Many of von Sanders' troops were peasant farmers who could not read or write. Like Hamilton, he lacked time to prepare. Unlike Hamilton, he did not dilly-dally. He ordered his troops to fortify the beaches with wood and wire. He scouted the

Australian and British Military Formations of 1915

Section: eight to 10 men, commanded by a corporal

Platoon: four sections, commanded by a lieutenant

Company: four platoons, perhaps 200 men, commanded by a captain

Battalion: four companies, around 1000 men, commanded by a lieutenant colonel or colonel

Brigade: four battalions, around 4000 men, commanded by a brigadier or brigadier general

Division: three brigades, commanded by a major general

Corps: three or four divisions, commanded by a lieutenant general

Army: four corps, commanded by a general

Light Horse: The Australian Light Horse was organised into regiments and brigades. A regiment was the rough equivalent of a battalion – consisting of four companies – except that its strength was nearer 500 men than 1000.

Turkish formations: The Turkish army at Gallipoli consisted of regiments rather than brigades. A division usually consisted of three regiments, each of three infantry battalions, plus artillery.

peninsula and tried to work out where the British invaders would land.

Hamilton's commanders did not like the landing plans but they went along with them. British troops would land on beaches at Cape Helles. The Anzacs would land on what would become known to the British as Brighton Beach, to the north of Gaba Tepe. Then they would stream across the plain beyond. But as we already know, the Anzacs landed in the wrong place.

CHAPTER FOUR

Courage Meets Chaos

Four months after the Gallipoli landing, the Turks captured two New Zealanders and questioned them. You live so far away, they said, why come here to fight? The Kiwis replied that they thought war would be like playing rugby.

Australians went to war with the same reckless spirit. Some Anzacs wrote letters from Egypt depicting battle as a romantic quest, dressing up death in ideas of honour and sacrifice. They brimmed with a pride normally reserved for an Ashes cricket victory. A Sydney Light Horseman admired the men's composure. 'The boys are talking like a lot of schoolkids, to see them one would think it was a picnic they were getting ready for,' he wrote. All this changed at dawn on 25 April.

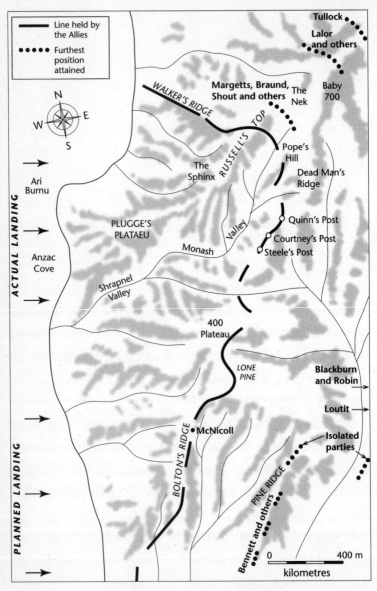

Line held by the Allies

Furthest position attained

Tullock

Lalor and others

Baby 700

Margetts, Braund, Shout and others

The Nek

WALKER'S RIDGE

RUSSELL'S TOP

Pope's Hill

Dead Man's Ridge

The Sphinx

Ari Burnu

PLUGGE'S PLATEAU

Valley

Quinn's Post

Courtney's Post

Steele's Post

Monash

Anzac Cove

Shrapnel Valley

400 Plateau

LONE PINE

Blackburn and Robin

Loutit

BOLTON'S RIDGE

McNicoll

Isolated parties

PINE RIDGE

Bennett and others

ACTUAL LANDING

PLANNED LANDING

0   400 m
kilometres

THE ANZAC FRONT-LINE, 25 APRIL 1915

Dawn, 25 April

The sun rose over the Sari Bair range and lit up a scene of chaos. Hamilton watched 'wave after wave of the little ants press up and disappear' from a battleship offshore. His plan was already doomed and the landing would be the smoothest part of the attack. A few hundred Anzacs were killed or wounded in the first hours. At least machine-guns did not cut them down as they waded to shore, as happened to the British at Cape Helles. There, the waves washed red with blood.

The Anzac plan was simple enough. A covering force of 4000 Anzacs would take three landmarks – the bald hill called Chunuk Bair to the north, Scrubby Knoll to the east, and Gaba Tepe to the south. With these positions secured, the main body would advance across the peninsula. The Anzacs were to capture a conical hill known as Mal Tepe and, later, the town of Maidos.

The script was tossed out at 4.29 am, when the Anzacs landed around 1.5 kilometres north of their intended landing site. The Turks expected an invasion, but they didn't foresee a landing in this untamed country. Had the Anzacs landed as planned, they would have rushed into barbed wire and machine-guns. At Anzac Cove, they stared up at hills that made no sense at all.

There was no pattern to the jagged cliffs and plunging valleys. The country was hopelessly eroded. The Anzacs didn't know where they were, what they were supposed to be doing, or where the enemy lurked. Their maps didn't show the quirks of this mad terrain. Steep hills led to sheer drops. Trails led to razorbacks.

The Anzacs' boats landed in a mixed-up clump rather than being spread over a broad front. Men in the same companies landed hundreds of metres apart. There was no room to untangle battalions. Some soldiers took a week to be reunited with their mates. The Anzacs were supposed to capture the third ridge of hills from the coastline in the first hours. They never did. Not that day. Not for the rest of the campaign.

They spent the first day fending off Turkish attacks here and rushing after Turks there. Most Anzacs were volunteers who had never faced fire. Fear, courage and bravado spilled over in the adrenaline rush. Men went left instead of right and right instead of left.

A Perth civil servant, Major A. H. Darnell, was the second-most senior officer in his battalion. He felt mad, wild and thrilled as he crawled uphill. Men fell around him. Only then did Darnell realise he had not drawn his revolver. Below, some Anzacs fired at the silhouettes of their countrymen on the skyline. They thought they were firing at Turks.

Some men rushed one and a half kilometres inland before daylight. The soldiers at first met little resistance. The 200 or so Turks who fired on the landing boats melted into the holly-like scrub. Some Anzacs thought the day was won by 6 am. Then shrapnel shells began bursting on Plugge's Plateau.

One battalion advanced towards 400 Plateau, to the right of where they had landed. Two others scaled the heights to the left. Small parties on both fronts crossed the second ridge of hills. Thousands of Turkish reinforcements massed a few kilometres inland. Soon enough, they rolled up in 'black clouds' over Scrubby Knoll on the right and down Baby 700 on the left. They screamed 'Allah' when they charged.

The air reeked of cordite, wild thyme and lavender. The sun shone, then drizzle fell. The Anzacs fired and dug, advanced and retreated, thirsted for water and the chance to lie down. Officers stood up to find their men, and bullets found them first. The officers were easy targets. Shoulder pips denoting their rank stood out like white spots from afar. From the start, no one was safe in the area that would come to be known simply as Anzac. Because of bursting shrapnel, the beach could be as deadly as the front-line.

Anzac Cove was congested with men, bodies, boats and supplies. Stragglers returned to the beach. New arrivals waited for orders that did not come. The wounded lay in lines. They cursed and groaned and died. Doctors scrambled to find boats to evacuate men to hospital ships. Two doctors tried to treat 850 wounded on one ship. Barges taking off the wounded became slippery with blood. Some ship captains refused to take the wounded because of overcrowding.

By every measure, the plan had failed. At 2 pm, about 4000 Turks fought 12 000 Anzacs. The wild terrain and Allied confusion evened the fight. Besides, the Turks had the high ground. The battle turned into a siege. The Anzacs couldn't get out. The Turks couldn't get in. It would stay like this for months.

By dark, about 2000 of the 16 000 Anzacs landed were dead or wounded. The survivors would never again confuse war with sport. 'How we prayed for this ghastly day to end,' an Australian soldier later said.

Today, thousands of Australians gather sand from Anzac Cove to take home. But to understand the origins of the Anzac story, we must scale the hills and peer into the valleys. That's where most of the killing went on – up on the second ridge. But no one can ever fully understand 25 April. That's because it was a shambles.

Private Arthur Blackburn, of Adelaide, was twenty-one and just out of law school. He sank under the water three times in struggling ashore. Men fell around him. He fixed his bayonet, then rushed on 'to drive the beggars away'. He wrote to his brother: 'The way our chaps went at it was a sight for the gods; no one attempted to fire but we just went straight on up the side of the cliff, pushing our way through thick scrub and often clambering up the steep sides of the cliff on all fours.'

Blackburn reached the top of the first ridge to the right of Anzac Cove and took cover. Turks fired from high ground about 100 metres away. Two men on his left and one on his right fell as daylight dawned. 'It is an absolute mystery to me how we ever lived through it, for frequently men would fire at us from not more than 10 or 20 yards away,' he wrote.

> However we pushed on, forcing our way through the scrub and clambered and crawled up the second ridge, only to again practically find no enemy in sight. The country suited them beautifully for they could crawl forward in front of us through the scrub, firing all the time and we could hardly ever see them.

Blackburn lost contact with his 10th Battalion mates. He had crossed through Shrapnel Gully, which would soon be clogged with Anzac troops. He now stood on 400 Plateau, a heart-shaped plain running roughly half a kilometre from north to south, and wrinkled by the odd gully and depression. Here he met up with Lance Corporal Phil Robin, a South Australian accountant.

Blackburn and Robin raced to the next ridge. A captain ordered them to scout ahead. They trekked south, towards Scrubby Knoll. The pair may have crossed the crest. They may have glimpsed the Dardanelles glistening in the sunlight. But there was no time to stare. Turkish reinforcements, roused from two hours' sleep, had rushed across the plain from

Maidos. They fired at the lonely pair of Australians. Blackburn and Robin hurried back to 400 Plateau, where the Australians had begun to dig in.

Several other small parties trekked ahead on the right, but they too were forced to retreat. It wasn't yet 8 am. Blackburn and Robin had scrambled to within 5 kilometres or so of the Dardanelles. It was the furthest inland the Anzacs would ever get. The 10th Battalion was supposed to take Scrubby Knoll. But soon the Turks set up headquarters there. Their guns looked over nearly all of Anzac. They could see every movement on 400 Plateau.

Blackburn was sent back for reinforcements and never saw Robin again. He won the Victoria Cross in France the following year and survived three years as a Japanese prisoner-of-war in World War Two. He had been at Robin's marriage to an English nurse, Nellie, just before sailing from Egypt. Robin was killed on 28 April. Nellie was pregnant. She and the baby died during the birth.

Blackburn and Robin were brave men – and their dashes showed up the Anzac muddle. No one followed the pair forward. Their commanders didn't know where they were. Other groups struck out, never to be seen again. We only know where they died because Australian officials found their remains – skeletons and rags – after the war had ended.

The Anzac commanders tried to advance but they couldn't establish a front-line. The first day became an exercise in plugging gaps. Troops in one valley did not know what troops in the next were doing. One unit surged and the next shied. Scraps broke out on one hill and all was quiet on the next.

As Major Walter McNicoll's 6th Battalion advanced, he smelt strange fragrances but 'no one stayed to botanise'. He ordered two companies, headed by his subordinate, Major Henry Gordon Bennett, forward from Bolton's Ridge. Soon Bennett's men were out of sight and McNicoll had a problem. His companies in the rear had been diverted to other emergencies. He had no one to help Bennett.

Shrapnel burst overhead and a pellet ripped the canvas of McNicoll's ammunition pouch. He found himself commanding a line from the southern edge of Plateau 400 to Bolton's Ridge. Small groups of soldiers approached him, asking what to do. They needed someone to lead them. Their officers were dead, wounded or plain lost.

'It was a case of a quick search for a man with "that narsty fightin' face that all nice people 'ate",' McNicoll wrote. 'A sharp order, "You take charge!" and they were off to join Major Bennett who was with the forward line until his second wound put him out of action for a while.'

400 Plateau, 3.30 pm

The order to dig in on Bolton's Ridge was given. Charles Bean wrote of five 'heroic but useless' Anzac advances on 400 Plateau in the first hours. Bean said the truth could never be fully told because most of the combatants lay dead.

Evacuation of the Wounded at the Landing

Arrangements for the evacuation of wounded during the landing were disastrous. There were not enough doctors or ships to handle the 2000-odd Australian casualties of that day or the many thousands wounded in the following days. Ships outfitted to carry troops and animals were forced to take on wounded. The *Galeka* prepared for 160 wounded, but took on 600 to 700 injured men. The *Lutzow*, with 160 horses aboard, had four bedpans for nearly 800 patients, and the only 'medical officer' aboard was a veterinary surgeon. The *Hindoo* was meant to deliver medical staff and equipment to the ships. Through administrative bungling, the ship lay idle off Cape Helles for four days.

Lance Corporal George Mitchell had been locked up for carousing in Egypt. Now he was trapped in a different sort of prison, on 400 Plateau. He lay in the scrub, pinned down by machine-gun fire. His renowned good cheer had deserted him. He could not lift his head, shout for help or dig into the reddish-brown earth. By late-afternoon, he welcomed a call to charge. He was ready to die.

'We rejoiced as we gripped our rifles,' he later wrote. 'The long waiting should be terminated in one last glorious dash, for our last we knew it would be, for no man could live erect in that tornado for many seconds.' The charge never happened, and Mitchell lived.

Lieutenant Margetts was trapped in skirmishes on and around a hill called Baby 700. The hill looked down on the valleys now teeming with Anzacs. The Australians had taken Baby 700 with few losses early in the morning. Some men smoked and joked while digging trenches at its base. Then Turk reinforcements crept forward. By day's end, Baby 700 had changed hands five times. Virtually every Anzac officer there, except Margetts, was dead.

On Russell's Top, below Baby 700, Margetts met Captain Joseph Peter Lalor and Captain Eric Tulloch. Lalor was the grandson of Peter Lalor, who led the gold diggers in the Eureka Stockade rebellion at Ballarat in 1854. He carried a sword and kept a whisky flask close. As a British historian later wrote, Lalor was 'colourful, even by Australian standards'.

Tulloch gathered about sixty men to capture Chunuk

Bair, one of the main Anzac objectives. The men scampered over Baby 700 and towards the next rise, Battleship Hill. About ten men fell as a machine-gun opened up from the right. They ran, then crawled, up Battleship Hill. Bullets chopped up the scrub around them. Twigs lodged under their collars and scratched down their backs. They faced fire from ahead, the left and right. Tulloch withdrew, but not before firing at a Turkish officer standing by a lone tree.

The officer did not move. We can't know for sure, but he was probably a divisional commander named Mustafa Kemal. Today, every Turkish banknote carries his image. Every village has a statue of him. To speak ill of his memory is against the law. Kemal survived the war to become Turkey's first president. He would be known as Atatürk, 'father of Turkey'. Kemal quashed the Anzac advances in the heights on the first day. His strategy was simple. Hurl the invaders into the sea.

It is said Kemal was woken early on 25 April and rode his horse towards the rattle of guns with a map and compass in his hand. He knew the Anzac country no better than the Australians. But Kemal recognised at once that to lose the heights was to lose the war. He gave his famous order: 'I do not order you to attack; I order you to die.'

Kemal's 57th Regiment blasted Margetts and his men off Baby 700. The Anzacs recaptured the hill. The Turks crept around the seaward flanks of the hill and sniped until the

Australians again backed off. But Margetts wasn't finished. At around 3.15 that afternoon, he led twenty men in a charge to take back the ground. His men lay in scrub so thick they couldn't see each other.

Most were killed or wounded. Those who survived baked in the heat and dreamt of a sip of water. Private R. L. Donkin, twenty-two, from the Hunter Valley, was shot twice in his left leg. A bullet pierced his hat and cut his hair. Another ripped his left sleeve. Three hit his ammunition pouches and blew up the bullets within. 'I know it's right and proper that a man should go back and fight again, but Sunday's battle and the horror of the trenches Sunday night . . . have unnerved me completely,' he wrote home.

Margetts survived. Exhausted but willing, he was about to chance his life in a fourth charge on Baby 700 when Lalor told him to return to the beach for stretcher-bearers. He was sniped at all the way and fell knee-deep in mud. Margetts lay down, 'utterly finished'. Lalor stood to rally his troops. 'Now then Twelfth Battalion –' he began. A bullet killed him in mid-sentence.

Tulloch's band had ventured about 3 kilometres from the beach. No Anzac would climb higher for more than three months. Baby 700 was lost.

To the right, on the rim of Monash Valley, Australians retreated to exposed spurs later named Pope's Hill, Quinn's Post and Courtney's Post.

The Turks rushed at the outposts again and again. Quinn's Post was at the apex of the Anzac triangle of land, and the key to the siege. The Turks attacked it from the front, its flanks, and from behind. Few thought the position could be held for more than a few days. The Anzacs there dug for their lives. They had nowhere to run to. Behind them were drops, some of them almost sheer, to the valley floor. This was the miracle performed by the Anzacs – holding onto positions as impossible as Quinn's.

CHAPTER FIVE

Digging In

The First Three Days

Kemal did not flinch when his 57th Regiment was wiped out on 25 April. He could find more martyrs. His men glimpsed the makeshift Anzac bases in Monash Valley and Shrapnel Gully from their perches at the Nek, and on Baby 700 above. They picked off water-carriers. They lobbed shells on troops waiting for orders. Turkish snipers camouflaged themselves and sneaked behind the Anzac lines. They would shoot hundreds over the next few weeks.

But Kemal demanded more. He wanted the invaders thrown back into the sea. If he tossed the Australians off Russell's Top, Pope's Hill and Quinn's Post, the Turks could

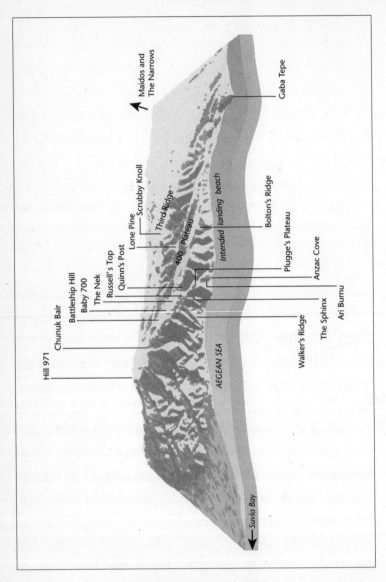

Maidos and The Narrows

Gaba Tepe

Scrubby Knoll

Third Ridge

Lone Pine

400 Plateau

Intended landing beach

Bolton's Ridge

Plugge's Plateau

Anzac Cove

Russell's Top

Quinn's Post

The Nek

Baby 700

Battleship Hill

Ari Burnu

The Sphinx

Walker's Ridge

Chunuk Bair

AEGEAN SEA

Hill 971

Suvla Bay

THE DIFFICULT TERRAIN OF ANZAC

then massacre the Anzacs near the beach. 'I must remind all of you that to seek rest or comfort now is to deprive the nation of its rest and comfort forever,' Kemal wrote to his troops.

The commander of the Australian 1st Division, General William Bridges, was slow to recognise Kemal's push on the left. Bridges had come ashore at 7.20 am on 25 April as shrapnel burst overhead. No one could explain to him what was happening. Bridges was forced to run an attack that he could not see or understand. Men, mules and supplies crammed the beach around his headquarters. Anzac Cove was clogged because it was smaller than the beach they were meant to land on.

Few things went right for the Anzacs. The evacuation of wounded held up the landing of soldiers. None arrived between 12.30 pm and 4 pm. An 'absolute minimum' of medical staff were on shore. There were so few stretchers that some stretcher-bearers had to piggy-back the wounded. Perhaps the shortage inspired John Simpson to use a donkey.

The landing of field guns was also delayed. Some mountain guns (the smallest artillery pieces used by the British army) were set up on 400 Plateau. Turks on Battleship Hill rained shrapnel on the guns. Blood flowed from the battery commander's head as he ordered a retreat. The British naval gunners couldn't fire because they didn't know where the Anzacs were. At 6 pm on the first day, only one 18-pounder field gun was onshore.

The Turks held a psychological advantage. They dropped shells on the Anzac position from Scrubby Knoll, Gaba Tepe and a battery near Chunuk Bair. Yet the Australians had virtually no shells to fire back at them.

Signalling systems to British ships broke down. Messages from the front were lost or confused. A 3rd Battalion officer, desperate for a machine-gun, resorted to wrapping his message around a stone and throwing it to the rear. He was so short of ammunition that he stripped the bodies of his dead mates for cartridges.

Pleas for reinforcements came in from fronts on the left and right. Bridges sent a reserve battalion to the right front, on 400 Plateau, late in the afternoon. The left front would have to sort itself out. Bridges had no more men to send – they were still at sea. Bridges' decision put Lieutenant Colonel G. F. Braund in a tight spot. Braund had given up the Nek when Turks rushed down the hill yelling 'Allah'. Yet his men held on at Russell's Top for the next three nights. Some historians say that their stand, alongside several New Zealand companies, saved the Anzac operation from buckling within hours.

The Anzac front-line gaped with holes – it was a series of shallow scrapes and rifle pits stretching from Walker's Ridge in the north, to Bolton's Ridge in the south. Plunging ravines were impossible to defend and Turks sneaked through the gaps on the first night. The entire front was about 2.5 kilometres long and about a kilometre from the Aegean Sea at

Quinn's Post, the innermost point. An Anzac commander called the position a 'cheesebite out of the cliffs'.

The confusing terrain meant both armies missed chances to break through the enemy's defences. The Anzacs held Lone Pine in the first few days but fell back when no reinforcements arrived. Concentrated Turkish attacks at Quinn's Post or Russell's Top would have overrun the Anzacs. Kemal attacked feverishly on the left of the Anzac front, but without a clear strategy. By the end of the first day, Turk casualties were said to be about 2000, or about one in three men.

At dusk on 25 April, Anzac looked like a cross between a shipwreck and a mining town. Troops scraped holes into the hillsides to fall into and sleep. Their dugouts looked like a cross between a grave and a cave. A few officers had biscuit boxes to sit on, and waterproof sheeting. The men on the front-line dug in the darkness. The Anzacs would live like rabbits for the next eight months. They would declare that the shovel was nearly as mighty as the rifle. The safest place was underground.

Dusk – Dawn, 25–26 April

Ellis Ashmead-Bartlett was a first-rate British journalist. He had stumbled into war zones since he was a teenager. He had built a fine career by reporting wars and cheating on his expenses. Ashmead-Bartlett's logical mind and loud mouth offended some British officers. He got things right too often. As we will see later, he helped to ensure that the Gallipoli campaign was called off. Before that, he accidentally started the Anzac legend.

His first article on the landing was published in Australian newspapers on 8 May. He wrote what a fretful nation yearned to hear. The 'raw colonial troops' were worthy of fighting alongside Allied heroes on the Western Front. 'Though many [Anzacs] were shot to bits, without hope of recovery, their cheers resounded through the night,' he wrote. 'They were happy because they knew they had been tried for the first time and not found wanting.'

People pasted the article in scrapbooks. Church ministers quoted it on Sundays. Between April and May, enlistments in Australia doubled, mainly because of exaggerated reports of glorious feats at Gallipoli. Reports from journalists in Athens suggested that the Allies were about to take the Dardanelles. No one at home knew that the Anzacs couldn't even take the next hill.

Today, parts of Ashmead-Bartlett's report on the landing sound absurd. He wrote a cooler account of events in his 1928 book, *The Uncensored Dardanelles*. In this, he wrote of landing at Anzac Cove at about 9.30 pm on 25 April.

[I] found myself in the semi-darkness amidst a scene of indescribable confusion. The beach was piled with ammunition and stores, hastily dumped from the lighters, among which lay the dead and wounded, and men so absolutely exhausted that they had fallen asleep in spite of the deafening noise of battle. In fact, it was impossible to distinguish between the living and the dead in the darkness. Through the gloom I saw the ghost-like silhouettes of groups of men wandering around in a continuous stream apparently going to, or returning from, the firing-line. On the hills above there raged an unceasing struggle lit up by the bursting shells, and the night air was humming with bullets like the droning of countless bees on a hot summer's day.

When Ashmead-Bartlett landed, he was accused of being a spy, mainly because he was wearing a peculiar green hat. Jumpy officers considered shooting him.

Ashmead-Bartlett met Sir William Birdwood, the British cavalryman who commanded the Anzac corps. The general asked him to deliver an important message to Hamilton, who was at sea.

Birdwood's note relayed reports from senior officers that men were dribbling back from the front-line. If Turkish shelling continued, 26 April could be a 'fiasco'. 'I know my representation is most serious but if we are to re-embark it must be done at once,' Birdwood wrote.

Birdwood asked Hamilton whether Anzac forces should

Horses, Mules and Donkeys

Nearly 8000 horses sailed from Australia with the first convoy in November 1914. Despite a six-week voyage in confined conditions, only 3 per cent died on the journey, not the expected 15–20 per cent. Some of the horses accompanied the troops to Anzac in April. But when the Australians did not advance as expected, very few horses were landed – they were unsuited to Gallipoli's harsh terrain. Most horses were returned to Egypt in early May.

Mules and donkeys were bought in Middle Eastern ports before the landing at Anzac. They were used to move supplies and ammunition and, occasionally, to ferry the wounded to the beach. They were in constant danger of death and injury from shellfire. In early May, one heavy bombardment on the beach killed thirty-four mules and fourteen horses. General Birdwood then ordered that supplies from the beach were only to be carried during the night.

be evacuated. He himself was shocked by the thought. But his subordinates, Bridges and Major General Alexander John Godley, the Englishman commanding the second Division, told him that front-line outposts needed more men and more artillery. Without these, was there much point in trying to hang on?

The Anzacs were exhausted after their first day of war. Many were brave, but many more were just confused. They still had much to learn. Some left the front-line to bring down their wounded mates. Others stayed at the front and endured a long night shooting at shadows.

Hamilton was asleep when Birdwood's note was delivered to him on the *Queen Elizabeth*. He wore pyjamas as he consulted his staff. They told him an evacuation might take three days. Hamilton didn't want to think too much about failure at Anzac. There was enough trouble with the British landings down south, at Cape Helles.

Hamilton suspected that he lacked the men or artillery to force the peninsula. But he was also a hopeless optimist. He sent Birdwood a cheery response. 'You have got through the difficult business, now you only have to dig, dig, dig, until you are safe,' he wrote.

26-28 April

Oliver and Joe Cumberland were in the 2nd Battalion, led by Lieutenant Colonel Braund. They charged up Walker's Ridge on 25 April and lay low in the cover of prickly dwarf oak. Oliver was shot. He told his sister he was charging a hill with his bayonet when a bullet ripped into his hip and grazed the bone.

On 8 May, recovering in a Cairo hospital, Oliver wrote: 'Una I don't know how Joe is at present, but he was not hurt when I left the field . . . Well dear Una don't worry . . . everything will come right in the end. The Turks are going to be smashed this time and it won't take long either.'

Oliver didn't know that Joe was already dead. We can only guess at Joe's whereabouts when he was wounded. All we know for sure is that the 21-year-old train driver was shot before 1 May.

Still in Egypt, Oliver found out about Joe's death, in late May: 'poor Joe is gone – he died of wounds in Alexandria hospital on fifth of May,' he wrote to his sister.

> I did not know until yesterday, I went to headquarters offices in Cairo and saw the list of killed and wounded. I had been very anxious wondering where he was, and when I saw the list I did not know what to do. I wandered about the streets nearly mad, I felt so lonely.

Joe might have been shot in Kemal's counter-attack of 27 April. The Australians had been expecting a rush since the grey morning of 26 April. Both sides were still making basic mistakes. On the second morning, the Anzacs advanced once again to the right, even though no advance had been ordered. Kemal had new troops to throw at the Anzacs. The Turkish commander issued a statement to his troops: all those not prepared to die would be shot.

Six lines of Turks rushed down Battleship Hill, like 'ants

on a disturbed nest'. The navy guns opened up and the attack was stalled. The Turks charged with bugles and bombs after dark, from Russell's Top to 400 Plateau. Machine-guns mowed them down. Eight Anzacs in a forward trench near Quinn's Post fired until their rifles were almost too hot to handle. They stopped a Turkish charge of 300 men. Ivor Margetts was under attack at Wire Gully. Near dawn, he fell asleep standing up. He still had his revolver in his hand.

Braund cried at the 2nd Battalion's roll-call after his men were relieved for the first time, on 28 April. Of the 968 who landed on 25 April, 450 of his men were now dead, wounded or missing. The 1st Australian Division had suffered one-in-three casualties. Of 5000 lost, only one soldier was taken prisoner. In the first days, both Anzacs and Turks killed many who surrendered.

Shell-shocked Anzac troops trudged back to the beach. Bean described them as 'tired children'. They fell asleep with food uneaten in their hands. Bean wrote: 'Bearded, ragged at knees and elbows, their puttees often left in the scrub, dull-eyed, many with blood on cheeks and clothes, and with a dirty field dressing round arm or wrist, they were far fiercer than Turks to look upon.'

In Margetts' battalion, only six of the thirty officers who landed remained.

For my own part I had no overcoat, my trousers were torn
in ribbons, and my boots were laden with mud, but,

nevertheless, dirty, weary and cold though we were, we had the satisfaction of knowing we had done what was asked of us. It was almost pathetic to see how one man would greet a pal who had been separated from him in the fight and whom he thought was either wounded or killed.

Braund liked to take short cuts through the scrub. An Anzac sentry shouted for Braund to identify himself six nights later. Braund was slightly deaf and did not hear him. The sentry shot him dead.

CHAPTER SIX

Life at Anzac

Sir Ian Hamilton marvelled at the spectacle when he landed at Anzac Cove for the first time, on 29 April. The cliffs looked too steep to climb, except that the cliff faces were 'pock-marked with caves like large sand-martin holes'. Swarms of bullets sang through the air and plopped into the sea. About 500 naked Anzacs swam and shouted and splashed. They did not seem to notice the bullets at all.

The behaviour of the Anzacs was considered peculiar from the first day. They fought well, but they were casual about protocol behind the front-line. The Australians delighted in embarrassing senior officers. Visiting British officers frowned when Anzacs failed to salute them. Even the

New Zealanders thought the Australians slovenly. Colonel William Malone, of the Wellington Battalion, couldn't wait to be moved away from them. 'They are like masterless men going their own ways,' he said.

The Anzacs used swear words as verbs, nouns and adjectives. Colloquialisms sprung up, such as 'dead-meat ticket' for an identity disc. Commander Charles Dix, who was in charge of landing the boats on 25 April, was widely known by Australians as that 'f–ing old bastard Neptune'. The Turks heard the word 'bastard' yelled so often, they assumed 'bastard' must be an Australian god.

Anzacs continued to lug water and ammunition as shrapnel pinged into piles of kerosene tins on the beach. Stretcher-bearers didn't slow for shrapnel storms. They rinsed their stretchers in the sea, then rushed off for the next bloodied soldier. No one took much notice of a cheery bloke with a cigarette hanging from the side of his mouth. Years later, at least a few Anzacs told fibs about their fine 'friend', Simpson.

A British officer described the Anzac attitude as 'absolute madness'. The Anzacs noted gory deaths in their diaries as everyday events. Sergeant Cyril Lawrence, an Australian engineer, was horrified when he saw a man's stomach blown out. Later, he saw worse and felt less. 'We received the same old shells today,' he wrote on 25 June. 'Russ and I went down to have a swim, and they opened up. It is marvellous how accurately they can place their shells. The first one got eighteen men. I must go down after dark.'

Colonel John Monash arrived with the Australian 4th Brigade early on 26 April to command at the hottest area of fighting, the rim of Monash Valley. He was struck by shrapnel as he collected his men but was unhurt. Monash was forty-nine and overweight, a society figure in Melbourne and a student of Napoleon's battles. He was an engineer who labored over details. He also had university degrees in arts and law. During lulls at Gallipoli, he played chess.

Monash saw order where others saw chaos. Latrines were yet to be set up. The unburied dead stank in front of the Anzac trenches. Ammunition-carriers, telephonists, digging parties, grave parties and periscope-hands ran about the place. 'Yet everything works as smoothly as on a peace parade, although the air is thick with clamour and bullets and bursting shells and bombs and flares,' Monash wrote.

The noises never stopped. Bangs, pops, fizzes and rattles. After a few weeks at Gallipoli, Monash and his men argued over the longest period of silence. Most felt ten seconds was the longest period. One man swore he'd counted fourteen seconds, but no one believed him. 'We are all of us certain that we shall no longer be able to sleep amid perfect quiet, and the only way to induce sleep will be to get someone to rattle an empty tin outside one's bedroom door,' Monash wrote.

Nurses

Hundreds of Australian nurses served overseas during the Gallipoli campaign, working in hospitals and on the hospital ships. Twenty-five of these nurses sailed with the first convoy in November 1914.

The women worked in horrific conditions. Hospitals were overcrowded. Men arrived with wounds that had been left untreated for days. One nurse on a hospital ship recorded, 'On some trips . . . we did at least 20 hours a day. I have found patients dead, perhaps for quite a time undiscovered.'

On the island of Lemnos, nurses ran short of water and tore up their clothes for bandages. In a diary entry dated 11 August 1915, Miss Grace Wilson, matron of the Lemnos hospital, describes the arrival of 400 soldiers to the island: 'Just lay the men on the ground and gave them a drink. Very many badly shattered . . . All we can do is feed them and dress their wounds . . . A good many died . . . could only wish all I know to be killed outright.' Ten days before, Wilson had learned of the death of one of her brothers, at Quinn's Post.

Anzacs clamber off
a transport ship at
Gallipoli, 25 April
1915.   (AWM J05589)

Many Australian units took mascots to Egypt.   (AWM C02588)

The Sphinx. (AWM C01488)

Anzac Cove. Note the naked swimmers. (AWM H03500)

Eager for news from Gallipoli, crowds gather outside the office of the *Argus*. (AWM H11613)

Wounded men, early May. (AWM C02679)

Winston Churchill, pictured here in France, drove the decision to invade Turkey. (AWM H12243)

Captain Phil Fry. A soldier sleeps in a dugout behind him. Fry was killed in a bayonet charge. (AWM A05401)

Packing cases serve as stairs for the steep climb up Pope's Hill.
(AWM H15375)

John Simpson Kirkpatrick, right, alongside a skeleton used to train stretcher-bearers at a Western Australia camp. (AWM A03116)

Anzacs wait for a letter – their only contact with the outside world.
(AWM P01116.047)

Private Oliver
Cumberland. (COURTESY
OF JOAN CROMMELIN)

Private Joe
Cumberland. (COURTESY
OF JOAN CROMMELIN)

Alfred Cameron, of the 3rd Light Horse, was
one of the few Aborigines to serve at Gallipoli.
(COURTESY OF THE SOUTH AUSTRALIAN MUSEUM)

Mustafa Kemal, later known as Atatürk, is credited with saving the Turkish position. (AWM A05319)

The wedding of Phil Robin, third from the right, and Nellie in Egypt. Behind Robin stands Arthur Blackburn. (COURTESY OF ROBIN ASHWIN)

Sergeant Cyril
Lawrence gets
a haircut.
(AWM P02226.020)

Historian Charles
Bean, front, and
British journalist Ellis
Ashmead-Bartlett at
Imbros, 1915.
(AWM A5382)

Night, 2 May

Hamilton's invasions at Anzac and Helles had stalled. The Anzacs were locked up in a fortress of gullies and cliffs. They dug trenches less than 1.5 kilometres from where they'd landed. Constantinople may as well have been on Mars. No longer did Anzacs lay bets on a likely arrival date. Even the first-day objectives looked impossible to take.

Lieutenant General Birdwood wanted to break the Anzac siege by recapturing Baby 700. Monash protested that the orders were half-baked but Major General Godley over-ruled him. Godley was from the English world of hunt-clubs and polo – the world of privilege. In 1915, such pursuits counted as credentials. Monash was only a civilian soldier.

Godley launched frontal charges from Russell's Top, Pope's Hill and Quinn's Post on 2 May. The attacks were supposed to be co-ordinated across the line but Godley's planning was shoddy. Troops charged in small groups after they had bunched up in Monash Valley and Shrapnel Gully.

A bombardment before the charges warned the Turks that the Anzacs were about to charge. Machine-gun fire ripped into the Anzacs as star shells burst overhead. Waiting Anzacs sang 'Tipperary' and 'Australia Will Be There'. Their cheers died out after about half an hour. New Zealanders who followed them fell dead two or three steps from the parapet.

Some troops scrambled about 100 metres and started

digging in at a maze of Turk trenches known as the Chessboard. By dawn they had been killed or forced back. British marines captured a ridge but were shot down when they reached its crest. Their bodies lay for days like 'ants shrivelled by a fire', until a marine climbed up after dark to kick them into the valley. The ridge became known as Dead Man's Ridge.

Monash had about 4000 soldiers under him when he landed on 26 April. Eight days later he had 1770. In his official report, Godley dressed up the assault as something grand. No ground had been gained. About 1000 Allied troops were killed or wounded. But Godley said the operation was 'very valuable in demonstrating to [the Turks] that our force was capable of determined offensive effort'.

The Battles of Krithia, 6–8 May

Walter McNicoll, the Geelong teacher and father of five, finally rested on the night of 28 April. He had spent hours chasing up the troops who advanced without orders on 26 April. Some of them didn't want to come back. Then the Turks counter-attacked the next morning. By the time McNicoll lay down on his greatcoat, more than 40 per cent of his 6th Battalion troops were listed as casualties. He woke to find himself lying in a puddle. He was too tired to care.

The 6th Battalion had been relieved by British marines.

The marines were young and afraid. They huddled in small groups and fired aimlessly. McNicoll was called back to the front-line because the marines had 'the jumps'. He chatted with the marine battalion's commander, Lieutenant Colonel Bendyshe. A marine began to stare at him.

McNicoll was unshaven and dirty. His tunic was torn, his face tanned. The marine decided McNicoll was a Turkish spy. The marine straightened, raised his rifle and fired at McNicoll. The bullet missed the Australian and killed Bendyshe. Chaos broke out. Shots were fired and McNicoll cut his hand fending off a bayonet. He was tied up, searched, blindfolded and marched away under armed guard. One of McNicoll's officers had to rescue him. Birdwood visited McNicoll the next morning to congratulate him on his lucky 'escape' from the British.

McNicoll was back fighting the real enemy a week later. The 6th Battalion, as part of the 2nd Brigade, was sent south to help the British break the siege at Helles. The British wanted to capture Achi Baba, a hill they mistakenly believed looked over the forts on the Dardanelles. Just below Achi Baba stood the Turkish village of Krithia.

The British commander at Helles, Lieutenant General Sir Aylmer Hunter-Weston, failed badly in the First Battle of Krithia, on 28 April. He didn't know what was happening and neither did his troops. Hunter-Weston was a product of the British class system, which saw men of limited ability, but the 'right' social background, being promoted far beyond the reach of their talents. He may have been a career army commander but his planning was invariably sloppy. He had a bushy moustache and an off-handed manner. A few months into the Gallipoli campaign, someone asked him about casualties. 'Casualties?' Hunter-Weston snarled. 'What do I care for casualties?'

Hamilton wanted what would become known as the Second Battle of Krithia to begin before dawn. Hunter-Weston preferred to attack during the day. Hamilton deferred to his subordinate.

The battle ran for three days, from 6 May. The Allies suffered more than 6000 casualties. They advanced about 550 metres. Hunter-Weston's battle plans failed, but he stuck with them day after day.

Anzac troops, as well as British and French (the latter wore white helmets and blue tunics, and charged with drums and bugles), fought in this battle. Late in the afternoon of 8 May, McNicoll and the Australian 2nd Brigade rushed through Turkish fire to what was named the Tommies' Trench, which ran across a low plain cracked with wide gullies.

McNicoll jumped up on the parapet to lead his men on. He suddenly slumped against a tree stump, as if breathless.

'Are you hit?' asked someone.

'Oh yes, but I think it's slight,' McNicoll replied.

McNicoll had a shoulder wound but he ignored it. He

blew his whistle and waved his arm for his men to follow. Turkish machine-guns peppered the troops from all sides. Bullets and shrapnel kicked up clouds of dust. The Anzacs couldn't see ahead but they kept running anyway.

A British major described the Turkish fire as one great concentration of hell:

> The machine guns bellowed and poured on them sheets of flame and of ragged death, buried them alive. They were disembowelled. Their clothing caught fire, and their flesh hissed and cooked before the burning rags could be torn off or beaten out . . . Not for one breath did the great line waver or break. On and up it went, up and on, as steady and proud as if on parade.

McNicoll was shot again about 230 metres out from the Tommies' Trench. The bullet entered his abdomen and travelled downwards to lodge at the top of his right thigh bone. He was one of 1000 men to fall in his brigade in little more than an hour.

In 1915, wounds such as McNicoll's were usually fatal. The cries of the wounded echoed as darkness fell. 'Many men had been hit before reaching the Tommies' Trench, and the calls of these, whenever they heard the voices or feet of passing men, naturally first attracted the bearers,' Charles Bean wrote. 'Meanwhile for 500 yards in front of that trench the wounded were lying far more thickly.'

Bean couldn't leave the wounded to die. The journalist

dragged in a soldier unable to crawl. He was then asked to take a message ahead. He'd crept about 200 metres when a cheerful voice called: 'Hullo, old man; you up here?' It was McNicoll. Bean coaxed two stretcher-bearers to help him carry McNicoll to safety. The bullet was later removed in a London hospital. When McNicoll awoke from surgery, the first thing he saw was the bullet wrapped in ribbon and hanging from the bedpost.

Bean journeyed back and forth among the wounded. He placed packs to shield them. They begged him for a sip of water. He gave a morphia lozenge to an Anzac shot through the intestines. For his seventh trip, he filled a petrol tin with water and offered sips around.

No dressing stations had been set up. Stretcher-bearers had to carry the wounded all the way to the beach. Those who survived the night on the battlefield mostly died soon after dawn. Bean was furious with the 'dull, stupid, cruel, bungling that was mismanaging the medical arrangements'.

The battle at Krithia was pointless. The Australian 2nd Brigade suffered more than one-in-three casualties. In the 6th Battalion, Major Bennett was the only combat officer who could still walk. Bean was recommended for a Military Cross. But his honorary rank of captain meant he could not receive bravery awards. Bean later wrote that he hadn't been brave. He simply could not stand by and do nothing.

Music for their Ears

General Godley, Commander of the NZ & Australian Division, enjoyed music, and insisted that army bands be brought over to Gallipoli. He felt that music would lift the spirits of the troops. A band would sit on a sheltered ledge of Chailak Dere and play for the pleasure of anyone passing by. At first the music was greeted with an outburst of fire from the enemy trenches, but the fire soon stopped. It seems it was a relief to the war-torn Turks too.

CHAPTER SEVEN

A Private and a General

Australian troops tensed up when the Australian 1st Division commander, General William Bridges, visited the front-line. He bullied soldiers with gruff orders, but that's not why troops became scared. Bridges acted as though bullets bounced off him. He stood where Turkish snipers could see him. He mocked those who hid when shells blew craters in the ground. On 26 April, Bridges stood on the skyline and snarled at McNicoll about the state of the trenches at Bolton's Ridge – they weren't deep enough.

'For goodness sake come down here sir,' a voice said. 'You'll be hit for certain.'

'Be damned,' Bridges barked back.

Bridges' staff officers warned him again and again. The inevitable happened. Bridges was shot on 15 May while walking through Monash Valley.

Sandbags were piled thickly at several spots in the valley. Screens of brushwood were set up. But Turkish snipers still found ways to fell up to twenty Anzacs a morning. Bridges lit a cigarette below Steele's Post and dashed from a wall of sandbags. The bullet struck two main blood vessels in his thigh. A nearby doctor clamped the artery and vein seconds before Bridges would have bled to death.

There were no blood transfusions in 1915 and no penicillin to treat infection. Wounds relatively easy to treat today were deadly then. Bridges' leg needed to be amputated but doctors thought the operation would kill him. Gangrene set in, turning the wound black and stinking. Bridges died of infection on 18 May. His body was shipped home to Australia. So too was Sandy, the horse he'd left behind in Egypt. Bridges' was the only Anzac body brought home. Of 121 000 horses sent overseas, Sandy is thought to be the only one to come home.

Newspapers devoted thousands of words to Bridges' death. A British officer was telling three Anzac troops that Bridges had been given a knighthood when one of the Australians chimed in: 'Have they? Well, that won't do him much good where he is now, will it, mate?'

The day after Bridges died, a short Englishman with blue eyes and stick-out ears led a donkey up Shrapnel Gully. John

Simpson Kirkpatrick, of the 3rd Field Ambulance, had missed out on breakfast that morning, but he wasn't too fussed. 'Never mind,' he said in a thick brogue. 'Get me a good dinner when I come back.'

Simpson never came back. He was hit in the heart, either by a bullet or shrapnel, and died close to the spot where Bridges was shot. In twenty-four days, Simpson had brought in about 300 soldiers, most of them with leg wounds. He was a lively soul and he was brave, although many Anzacs matched that description in those first weeks. He whistled and sang. No one told him to use a donkey. He just went and did it.

The men called him Simmo, Simmie, Murphy and Scotty, but few knew him well. His donkey had more than one name, too – including Duffy, Murphy and Abdul – though he may have used more than one. It's said that Simpson spoke to his donkey in a mixture of Arabic swear words and Australian slang.

Few Anzacs mentioned Simpson's death at the time, although Colonel Monash wrote that Simpson's rescues earned the admiration of everyone at the upper end of Monash Valley. In life, Simpson was a nobody. It was two months after his death before Australia heard about him. Soon Simpson would be better remembered than Bridges, even though Simpson was a private and Bridges a general.

Simpson's tale took off with the public back home. It was an affecting story. Simpson was a Christ-like figure. He didn't kill anyone. He helped the weak. Recruiters used Simpson's story to encourage men to enlist. A film was made about him. Statues were built. There were poems and postage stamps. A few Anzacs rewrote their diaries to say they had met him. If Simpson's name became famous at Gallipoli, it was likely men heard about him in letters from home.

Now, every Australian schoolchild learns Simpson's story. Virtually all visitors to Gallipoli see his headstone at Beach Cemetery. It lies near the entrance and is often covered with flowers. There is always dirt rubbed into the inscription – so the words can be clearly read. In 2000, a group of twelve girls was seen gathering around the headstone. One began to weep. Soon they were all weeping.

We remember Simpson's feats at Gallipoli even though there were sadder deaths and bigger tragedies. Some still lobby for Simpson to be given the Victoria Cross. Yet Simpson the legend and Simpson the man are not the same thing.

The folklore is simple and straightforward. For forty years, until his letters were published, most assumed Simpson was a 'six-foot Australian'. Even his first biographer cheated with the facts. The truth about Simpson's life is more interesting than the myth.

Simpson's mother, Sarah, and sister Annie called him Jack. He had a tough life growing up near the docks in South Shields, in northern England. He left school at the age of twelve, to drive a milk cart. At seventeen, two days after his father was buried, and against his mother's wishes, Jack sailed to Australia.

Jack carried a swag and worked in canefields and coal mines, and as a ship's stoker. He tried riding horses on a cattle station but hated it. He lived in boarding houses and spent his meagre earnings on Woodbine cigarettes and lottery tickets. He sent as much pay home as he could spare, a pound here, 15 shillings there. Jack considered himself the head of the family, even after he had been away for more than five years.

In his letters, Jack's tone was sometimes playful and caring. He teased Annie about boyfriends. But Jack could be bossy too. He had a short fuse and forceful opinions. When his mother evicted a lodger, he wrote: 'I would have made that Russian Jew bugger dance a hornpipe on his ars [sic]'.

Jack wrote about brawling on a ship he was working on. At a Christmas Day lunch at sea off Western Australia, his drinking mate suggested they fight the sailors. 'You couldn't see anything for blood and snots [sic] flying about until the mates and engineers came forward,' Jack wrote. Another time, a drunk man hit him over the head with a poker. Jack broke a chair over the man's head.

Although his wanderings in Australia made for 'about the best life a fellow could hope for', Jack's heart belonged to the grime of northern England. He jumped ship and enlisted under his mother's maiden name, in Fremantle, Western

Australia, three weeks after war was declared. Jack was patriotic but he also wanted a free voyage home. He organised for 14 shillings a week – one third of his army pay – to go into a London bank account for his mother.

Jack was frustrated when the troops landed in Cairo – 'this Godforsaken place' – but hoped he was headed for France or England when they left on 28 February. On 10 May 1915, Annie and Sarah received their last correspondence from Jack. The field postcard was similar to a multiple-choice test. Jack crossed out the alternatives to leave a single line: 'I am quite well.'

Jack's mother waited anxiously for a letter from her son. She had lost three sons to scarlet fever. She could not bear to lose another. Annie wore a brooch fashioned from a medical corps badge. On 15 June 1915, she sent Jack a box of cigarettes. 'We would like a few lines in your handwriting if you could spend the time dear Jack,' she wrote. 'Goodnight lad & God protect you for your poor old Mother's sake for Oh Jack! how we do love you.'

Annie wrote three letters that were never answered. They were returned to her. Scribbled across one envelope was a single word: 'Killed'.

Jack was dead at twenty-two. But Simpson would live forever.

CHAPTER EIGHT

Play Ya Again Next Saturday

3.20 am, 19 May

The Australians knew they were coming. Something was up when the Turkish fire slowed the day before. Naval planes confirmed that long columns of Turks were marching towards Anzac. Now soldiers could see Turkish bayonets gleaming in the trenches opposite. Between 30 000 and 40 000 Turks would try to drive 12 500 Anzacs into the sea.

The Australians stood waiting shoulder-to-shoulder, wrapped in greatcoats. Lieutenant General Birdwood admired his Anzac troops in attack, but wondered whether they might be too casual in defence. He shouldn't have worried.

The Turks charged all along the front-line with bayonets

and bombs. A Turkish band played military tunes. There were only 4.5 metres between the Anzac trenches and the Turks' at Quinn's Post and Steele's Post. Over to the right, the gap was around 180 metres, over flat ground and through low scrub whittled down by rifle fire.

The Turks did not target weak points. They would have broken through if thousands had charged at Quinn's or Pope's Hill. The Anzacs sat and stood on top of the parapets, firing until their rifles burned hot. They reloaded magazines as fast as they could. It was estimated that they fired 950 000 rounds.

Hollering Turks made at least five charges at Quinn's Post and at least two on 400 Plateau. Anzac machine-guns blew gaps in the rushing wall of bodies ahead. They couldn't miss. Some Anzacs waved their hats. 'Play ya again next Saturday,' a 3rd Battalion soldier shouted. An Anzac officer, Lieutenant Jack Merivale, later wrote to his mother that defending the Anzac position was more fun than shooting wallabies.

Private Murray Aitken's platoon was supposed to play a supporting role only. The young accountant ignored orders and clambered forward. 'We got up to all sorts of dodges to get in and into all sorts of positions to have a shot,' he wrote. 'I forgot to take cover and did not notice the shrapnel while the bloodlust was on me . . . I'll admit to a certain savage pleasure in firing to kill.'

Turks threw 'football' bombs and a group of them took part of Courtney's Post. But they were trapped. While three

Australians distracted Turkish soldiers, Private Albert Jacka, a 22-year-old forestry worker from Victoria, climbed into no-man's-land and jumped the Turks from behind.

Jacka was lucky to be alive. A few weeks earlier a shell had exploded near his dugout. The officer lying next to him was killed but Jacka was untouched. Now he dived into the trench, shot five Turks and bayoneted two. The other Turks ran away. Lieutenant K. G. W. Crabbe found Jacka moments later. Turkish and Australian bodies lay around him. There were said to be twenty-six Turkish rifles in the trench. An unlit cigarette hung from Jacka's mouth. 'I managed to get the beggars, sir,' he said.

Jacka was soon evacuated with diarrhoea brought on by bad food and woeful sanitation. While he was recovering on Imbros, Jacka learnt that he was the first Australian to win a Victoria Cross at Gallipoli. VC winners received town parades and lavish newspaper profiles. Jacka became a national hero. Melbourne bookmaker John Wren honoured a promise to pay the first VC winner 500 pounds – enough money to buy a house. Jacka was later twice awarded the Military Cross in France.

The Turkish charge was doomed before sunrise. About 3000 lay dead all along the Anzac line. Another 7000 were wounded. The Anzacs suffered less than 800 casualties, including 160 dead. The failed charge confirmed what both sides already suspected. The Turks couldn't drive the Anzacs into the sea. But the Anzacs couldn't break out of their fortress. The defender would always hold off the attackers. The crazy landscape would always win.

The Pet Sniper

William Edward 'Billy' Sing, of the 5th Light Horse Regiment, was the crack sniper at Anzac. Sing was officially credited with shooting 150 Turks, although the true figure was probably more than two hundred. General Birdwood called Sing his 'pet sniper'.

Born of an English mother and a Chinese father, Sing grew up in Queensland. One of his 'spotters', Ion Idriess, described him as a small, dark man with a black moustache and a goatee beard. Idriess said Sing worked like a cat staking out a wall of many mouseholes.

Sing's number of 'kills' was followed closely by the other troops. Every morning before dawn, Sing and his spotter would move into a hidden position, scanning the opposing enemy trenches through a telescope. Any Turk who lingered at a loophole, or took careless peeps over the trench, became a target for Sing's deadly aim.

On one occasion Sing shot a Turk when General Birdwood was acting as his spotter. Sing told Birdwood that the kill could not be added to his score as he had been aiming at a different Turk.

Sing received the Distinguished Conduct Medal for conspicuous gallantry at Anzac. He served in France with the 31st Battalion, and died alone in Brisbane in 1943.

Until now, the Anzacs had believed that the Turks muti-lated the Australian dead. Yet with Turks dead and moaning only a few metres away, the Australians saw up close that the 'mutilations' of their mates had been caused by machine-gun fire. Flesh was pulped. Limbs dangled by threads. Bean saw Turkish bodies with head wounds big enough to fit a hand through. Flies swarmed over piles of bodies as the sun burned down. The bodies had to be buried before disease broke out. That's why a truce was called.

24 May, Truce

Turks and Anzacs covered their noses, shook hands and exchanged cigarettes in no-man's-land. Up to 4000 bloated and black bodies lay around them, many of them face down. For nine hours no guns rattled and no shells whined. Turks and Anzacs rolled up their shirtsleeves and dug graves for the dead.

Drizzle fell and men swooned. A British officer, Compton Mackenzie, a famous novelist, wondered why he was offered a cigar when he climbed up to Quinn's Post. The smell of death wafted down, so pungent he felt he could almost see it. Then he understood why he needed the cigar.

Arranging a truce was a delicate matter. Both sides feared appearing weak. A few days earlier, without warning, a few Turks had raised a white flag and begun to clear the dead and wounded in front of their trenches. General Harold Walker joined then in no-man's-land. He told them to send an officer under a white flag to arrange a formal truce so both sides could bury their dead.

The officer shared cigarettes with Australian officers when he arrived on horseback the next morning. He was blind-folded and carried to headquarters. During negotiations an Anzac cook was said to have poked his head into the tent and asked: 'Heh! Have any of you muckers pinched my kettle?'

Lines of enemy sentries faced each other for the truce. White flags were pegged at intervals. The clusters of officers reminded Mackenzie of officials at a sports day. An Australian suggested Mackenzie move his foot. 'Looking down I saw squelching up from the ground on either side of my boot like a rotten mangold the deliquescent green and black flesh of a Turk's head,' he wrote. '. . . I cannot recall a single incident on the way back down the valley.'

The bodies reminded one corporal of mowed hay. An Australian private grabbed a corpse by the arm and the arm came off in his hand. A Turkish-speaking British officer, Aubrey Herbert, was in charge of the operation. He held anti-septic wool, heavy with scent, to his face. He looked down on entire companies that had been slaughtered, 'not wounded but killed, their heads doubled under them with the impetus of their rush and both hands clasping their bayonets'. Herbert stood with a Turkish captain. 'At this spectacle even the most gentle must feel savage, and the most savage must weep,' the Turk said.

Both sides broke the strict conditions of the armistice. Australians took photos, even though cameras were banned. They buried men in the craters and gullies used as cover by Turkish snipers and bombers. Both sides surveyed each other's trenches. It was suspected that the Turks studied the weaknesses of Quinn's Post, and that this prompted a Turkish battalion to attack the position five days later. They nearly got it, too.

At 4 pm, the Turks came to Herbert for orders. He retired both Turkish and Anzac troops. He joked with the Turks that they would shoot him the next day. 'God forbid,' they said. The Australians shook hands with the Turks and said: 'Goodbye, old chap. Good luck.'

A Turk responded: 'Smiling may you go and smiling come again.'

Neither side fired for twenty-five minutes. The Turks and Anzacs had discovered that they liked each other. They would still fire at anything that moved in the enemy trenches, of course. And no one forgot the need to kill the enemy before he killed you. But from then on, few Anzacs described the Turks as savages any more. In their diaries, they began calling Johnny Turk brave and fearless.

Both sides still threw bombs into the other's trenches. But they began throwing cigarettes too, and milk and jam, although the Turks returned the tins of bully beef. An unusual camaraderie grew. It was as though the Anzacs and Turks felt that they should suffer the hardships of war together.

A Turkish Letter

The following letter was found on the body of a dead Turkish soldier. An Anzac soldier, Lieutenant H. R. McLarty, recorded it in a letter home, in July 1915.

To my dear husband,

Hussein Aga, I humbly beg to inquire after your blessed health. Your daughter sends her special salaams, and kisses your hand. Since you left I have seen no one. Since your departure I have had no peace. Your mother has not ceased to weep since you left. We are all in a bad way. Your wife says to herself, 'While my husband was here we had some means, since your departure we have received nothing at all'. Please write quickly and send what money you can . . . May God keep you and save us from the disasters of this war.

Your wife

Fatima

CHAPTER NINE

Flies and Bully Beef

June and July

Colonel William Malone, the strong-willed New Zealander, took over command at Quinn's Post on 9 June. Bodies lay broken and pulped in front of the sandbags. To try to remove them was to risk joining them. One corpse rotted so badly that a soldier set fire to it. The Anzacs on the escarpment lived, ate and slept with the smell of roasted flesh for days. The Turks probably smelt it, too. After all, they were so close that the Anzacs could hear them cough. The Turks dug tunnels and tried to blow up the Anzac trenches from below. They threw bombs, yelled and fired at anything that moved. The Anzacs did the same back.

General Hamilton watched a silent stream of men, all

bandages and blood, wander down from Quinn's in late May. They were victims of Turkish bombs. Troops below looked up at the outpost as they might a haunted house. 'Men lived through more in five minutes on that crest than they do in five years of Ballarat or Bendigo,' Hamilton wrote.

The Australians seldom wore shirts off-duty. They looked 'Turkish', as one journalist put it, with their thick stubble and dark tans. Malone was different. He rationed his water so that he bathed half his body a day, the other half the next. He washed his socks in the water left over. He ordered his men to be like cats and clean up after themselves. For every Turkish bomb thrown, two were to be thrown back.

Malone gave Phillip Schuler, a young journalist from the *Age,* a tour of Quinn's. It was as though Malone was showing off home renovations. Schuler marvelled that the maze of trenches, burrows, secret tunnels and deep shafts had not crumbled away. The neighbouring posts were just as shaky. Pope's Hill had to be pasted back together with sandbags after each night's shelling.

Malone replaced the haphazard dugouts on the slopes behind Quinn's with covered terraces. He put up wire netting to catch the 'cricket ball' bombs the Turks rolled down the slope. Malone guided Schuler through zig-zagging front trenches where the pair were exposed to enemy fire. 'Now we have given them a sporting chance to snipe us, let us retire,' Malone said. 'I always give a visitor that thrill.'

Malone was the fussiest housekeeper at Anzac. Who else

would have thought about planting roses? Other commanders tried to improve their sections of the line. Smart soldiers scrounged what they could. Corrugated iron for shelter. Greatcoats to sleep under. Biscuits boxes for tables. They were preparing for the long stay ahead. Everyone accepted that this triangle of miserable dirt was now their home.

Swimming

Swimming in the sea was popular with the men at Anzac, particularly as their daily water allowance left little for washing either themselves or their clothes. As the weather turned hot, the beach sometimes looked like a holiday resort. The Turks began lobbing shells into the sea amongst the bathers, but the men continued to swim there.

General Birdwood enjoyed a swim when possible. In the water, naked like everyone else, he was sometimes mistaken for a lowly private. Journalist Phillip Schuler wrote that one day a canvas pipe from a water-barge fell into the sea. The barge-man, not recognising the general, yelled at him: 'Well lend a fellow a ------ hand to get the ------ thing up.' Birdwood did not punish the barge-man for his rudeness. Rather, he helped out and later delighted in re-telling the story.

Occasional skirmishes broke out, including a suicidal Turkish charge at the Nek on 30 June. But June and July were relatively quiet months at Gallipoli. Both sides had suffered severe losses in frontal charges. Anzac artillery gunners couldn't do much – they were rationed to firing two shells a day. The Turks, too, lacked ammunition. After June 30, they didn't launch another major frontal attack at Anzac.

The Anzacs grew weary of fatigue duties. The sun burnt hotter and a plague of flies arrived. The troops lugged water and supplies up and down the hills and gullies. When they weren't lugging, they dug trenches or graves or tunnels. Trenches grew longer and deeper on either side of no-man's-land. Piles of yellow and orange clay mounted. No-man's-land was mostly bare, the scrub all shot away. Here and there lay the corpses of Turks and Anzacs who had been shot since the truce.

On the beach, men filled jam tins with nails, stones and barbed wire. These bombs were unpredictable, but better than nothing. Other work parties built periscope rifles. Devised by Lance Corporal W. C. B. Beech, the contraption allowed men to fire without exposing themselves. Framed in wood, a mirror was propped over the lip of the trench. The rifleman then lined up the rifle sights with another angled mirror that he peered at below.

The Anzac trenches were dug to a depth of about 2.5 metres. They were built dog-legged, so that Turks could not shoot right along the line if they seized a section. Communications trenches joined front and rear trenches, and steps were built into the walls of the front trench for firing over the parapet. Both Turks and Anzacs dug saps – trenches running longways to the front-line – that reached out into no-man's-land. At night they tried to join the saps to form a new front-line.

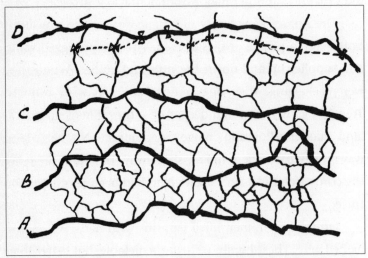

FOUR LINES OF TRENCHES AT LONE PINE, AS DRAWN BY SERGEANT CYRIL LAWRENCE. THE THIN LINES ARE COMMUNICATION TRENCHES. MARKED NEAR THE TOP IS THE LINE OF AUSTRALIAN OUTPOSTS AFTER THE ATTACK. A, B, C AND D REPRESENT THE ANZACS' LINES OF DEFENCE.

Both sides dug tunnels to blow up enemy positions from below. The tunnellers led dangerous lives. When they overheard enemy tunnellers tapping a few metres away, they raced to blow up the Turks before the Turks blew up them. Sergeant Cyril Lawrence led a small team that helped dig 2.4 kilometres of tunnels that extended in front of the most important post on 400 Plateau, Lone Pine. His men unearthed pottery from an ancient city. They dug around bodies or removed them. 'They have a peculiar smell of oily fat flesh,' Lawrence wrote.

Infantry troops generally worked 24-hour shifts in the front-line, twenty-four hours on fatigue duties and twenty-four hours in support trenches. They slept wherever they could, usually in dugouts knocked into the trench walls. They had to cook their own rations and collect their own firewood. Water was always scarce at the front. It had to be delivered from ships and carried from the beach. Wells were dug and tanks set up in outlying areas. Carriers had some of the most dangerous work of all.

Up to 600 shells a day fell out of the sky, when ammunition was in supply. The Turks always fired at dinnertime, when the Anzacs brewed their billies over small fires. Lawrence was once digging 50 metres inside a tunnel when a shell exploded at the tunnel mouth. He clambered out to discover that the Anzac guarding the tunnel had been decapitated. The poor man still had his hands in his pockets. 'Good God, I never want to see such a sight again,' Lawrence wrote.

Troops hunkered in caves dug into the sides of Monash Valley and Shrapnel Gully when shrapnel storms hit. Handmade signs directed visitors to stay to the left or right, to avoid snipers' bullets. Lonely wooden crosses marked solitary graves. A Light Horseman, Ion Idriess, was walking to the beach for water one day when a young man with snowy hair stepped out in front of him. 'Just as we were crossing Shrapnel Gully he suddenly flung up his water bottles, wheeled around and stared for one startled second, even as he crumpled to my feet,' Idriess wrote. 'In seconds his hair was scarlet, his clean white singlet all crimson.' Idriess would go on to become one of Australia's best-loved writers in the middle decades of the century.

Once, a shell exploded over a latrine where a line of men sat 'like a lot of sparrows on a perch'. The men scampered, their pants still around their ankles. 'The roar of laughter that went up could have been heard for miles,' wrote Lawrence. 'It's only these little humorous happenings that keep things going here.'

Funeral services were mostly conducted at night, for safety. One day a chaplain was mid-way through a burial when a nearby shell threw dirt on the party. 'Oh, Hell!' said the chaplain. 'This is too ho-at for me! I'm aff [sic].'

Death became a way of life. Troops could never escape its sights and smells. Many struggled with the nervous strain. Some became convinced that the next shell would kill them. Private Jack Gammage, a country kid from New South Wales, lost his nerve in June. He felt like every day was his last. By July, he didn't care whether he lived or not. Gammage endured to fight bravely two weeks later in the most terrible battle of Gallipoli, and he lived.

Private Victor Nicholson was under Malone's command at Quinn's. He saw a friend shot through the eye. Nicholson wanted to cry but feared he would never stop. 'There were friends going every day and sometimes every hour of the day, wonderful friends,' he wrote. 'I grieved inwardly. That was all you could do. As a war went on you could forget the death of a very fine friend in five minutes.'

A young West Australian bushman, Private Albert Facey, was more honest than most. In his autobiography, *A Fortunate Life*, he recalled charging in bayonet attacks at Gallipoli and expecting to die in all of them. 'The awful look on a man's face after he has been bayoneted will, I am sure, haunt me for the rest of my life,' he wrote. 'I will never forget that dreadful look. I killed men too with rifle fire – I was on a machine gun at one time and must have killed hundreds – but that was nothing like the bayonet.'

After a fearful shelling, a doctor prised shrapnel from Facey's jaw – after much pulling – and suggested further treatment on a hospital ship. Instead, Facey had teeth pulled on the beach, without anaesthetic. Why did he stay? To be with his mates. 'A sort of love and trust in one another developed in the trenches,' he wrote. 'It made us all very loyal to each other.'

Facey was one of three brothers who landed at Gallipoli. Facey's eldest brother, Joseph, died defending an outpost. Another brother Roy, was killed by a shell the day before he was to transfer into Facey's unit. Facey helped bury him. 'Roy was in pieces when they found him,' he wrote. 'We put him together as best we could – I can remember carrying a leg – it was terrible.'

Lice, Letters and the Gallipoli Trots

Lice as big as grains of wheat burrowed under clothes. Men tried burning and drowning them but the lice appeared to be both water- and fire-proof. 'The isolation in the trenches, and being confined to one area, was hard to take,' Facey wrote. 'It wasn't so bad when there was action, but living day in and day out almost underground and being lousy all the time got us down.'

Temperatures soared into the thirties. Flies buzzed on every corpse and every piece of food. They became more frustrating than the Turks. When a jam tin was opened, the jam became a 'blue-black mixture of sticky, sickly flies'.

'The flies are simply unbearable,' wrote Private Cecil McAnulty. 'They are here in millions, from the size of a pin's head to great bluebottles that bloated they can't fly. Other vermin irritate us very much at night & it is very troubled and restless sleep we get, when we get any at all.'

The food was awful and unvaried. Occasionally the men received a strip of fatty bacon or a serve of mushy vegetables. Condensed milk was a special treat. The beef was salty and made the men even more thirsty. Biscuits had to be soaked for hours to be softened. The outside would be scraped off, then the biscuit returned for more soaking. Many broke teeth on these biscuits.

The Anzacs received as little as one pint – about half a litre – of water a day, for drinking and bathing. Most drank the water and risked death from shellfire while bathing in the sea.

Lieutenant General Birdwood tried to take a dip each night, and he got around to see Australian troops every day. He struggled to grasp their dark wit but did nothing when they forgot to salute him. Birdwood's mingling reminded the soldiers that Anzac was miserable for generals as well as privates.

A delivery of mail was one of the few pleasures available, along with a swim in the sea, to the men on Gallipoli. Isolated from family and friends, and from news of the outside world, men read and re-read their letters, or shared the contents with their mates who had missed out.

Newspapers, often months old, were hungrily scanned for items of interest. Lieutenant H. R. McLarty hadn't washed for a week or taken his boots off for two when he received two newspapers and seven letters in one delivery. He felt like the 'the happiest man alive'. Soldiers' diaries show that a letter from home could lift the spirits of the most despondent of men.

The first mail arrived at Anzac a week after the landing and was then delivered about once a fortnight. Sometimes

Food and Water

Daily rations for the Anzacs during May included:

Preserved meat	12 ozs	**Tea**	⁵⁄₈ oz
Biscuits	1 lb 4 ozs	**Sugar**	3 ozs
Bacon	4 ozs	**Jam**	¼ lb
Cheese	3 ozs	**Salt**	½ oz
Onions	½ lb (or potatoes ½ lb, onions ¼ lb)	**Pepper**	¹⁄₃₆ oz

Lime juice was issued if potatoes and onions were not available. From June, the Anzacs received bread every second day if the weather permitted delivery. Fresh beef was obtained from refrigerated ships at Imbros, but it often arrived at Anzac flyblown or 'off' due to the heat. Occasionally the men received eggs, dried fruit, tinned stew, tinned milk and rum. The soldiers regularly received tobacco.

Water was always scarce at Anzac. Barges delivered water to storage tanks on the beach, and wells were sunk within hours of the landing. The men rarely received the recommended minimum of one gallon a day. By late July an old steam engine and pumping plant were installed on the beach and water was piped to outlying tanks. More than one hundred men with ropes were needed to haul the tanks into position. When the steam engine broke down, mules were used to carry water.

Turkish Food Rations

The Turks had porridge for breakfast, cheese for lunch, with olives on alternate days. They had white beans for dinner, with the occasional serving of onions and a little meat. A daily ration of a kilo of bread was provided. As the weather turned cold, raisins were sometimes substituted for the cheese. Coffee and tea were both scarce.

more than 1300 bags of mail would arrive. Inevitable delays occurred, particularly with parcels, or when a soldier was taken to hospital, or when soldiers had the same name. Later, newspapers were held for distribution to hospitals, which meant the troops missed out. General headquarters published a regular news-sheet, *The Peninsula Press*, to keep the men informed of events and to quell the many rumours that circulated.

In the late afternoon, many Anzacs briefly shut out the din of war. They gazed at the sunset over the jagged peaks of the islands of Imbros and Samothrace. 'The sea is nearly always like oil and as the crimson path streams across the water the store ships, hospital ships, torpedo boats and mine sweepers stand out jet black,' Cyril Lawrence wrote. 'God, it's just magnificent.'

The Australians brought no dental corps. Rotten and broken teeth caused hundreds of evacuations. Some men had teeth pulled by amateurs with blacksmith's pliers. Lawrence had a tooth pulled and realised it was the wrong one when the pain persisted a few days later.

The Indian Camp

Phillip Schuler wrote a vivid description of the Indian troops' camp at Anzac: 'A mass of rags and tatters it looked, for it was exposed to the fierce sun, and when gay coloured blankets were not shielding the inmates of the dugouts, the newly washed turbans of the Sikhs and Mohammedans were always floating in the idle breeze. Their camp was always busy. They never ceased to cook. Though the wiry Indians could speak little English, they got on well with the Australians, who loved poking about amongst their camps hunting for curios, while the Indians collected what trophies they could from the Australians.'

The most serious health problem was dysentery, the main symptom being chronic diarrhoea. By August, four in five Anzacs were struck down by the 'Gallipoli Trots'. Three quarters of the 1400 weekly evacuations were for illness rather than wounds. British officers had initially marvelled at the Anzac physique, likening the strapping troops to Greek gods. By July, the Anzacs trudged like walking scarecrows. Their dark skin hung loose on their wasted bodies.

The Anzacs' battle against weakness sapped them more

than enemy fire. 'It's absolutely piteous to see great sturdy bushmen and miners almost unable to walk through sheer weakness, caused by chronic diarrhoea, or else one mass of Barcoo rot [skin infection],' Lawrence wrote. 'We are all the same, all suffering from sheer physical weakness and yet we can't get relieved.'

Lawrence despised the 'damn wasters' at home who had not enlisted. 'Surely they won't ask this crowd to do another advance,' he wrote in August. 'Anyhow, I don't think that they could do it; they are too weak.'

He was wrong. Four days later, the Anzac generals ordered a huge attack. They were going to try to break out of their Turkish jail.

Turkish Divisional Orders (some time in July): 'The Australian and New Zealand Army Corps is approaching the limits of its resources. Most of the men have no clothing at all, except trousers, and even these are now being cut into pieces, so that one pair of trousers is sufficient for four men.'

AN ILLUSTRATED PAGE FROM *THE ANZAC BOOK*

CHAPTER TEN

Best Laid Plans

Breaking the Stalemate

The Anzac triangle had been locked in a stalemate for months. The Anzacs couldn't break out. The Turks couldn't break in. Now it was high summer – a blazing sun, gorgeous sunsets, no rain, lots of dust. Life was bearable, just. But the Anzacs knew they couldn't hang on once winter came. They would freeze in the snowstorms – many no longer owned a pair of long trousers. And rain would flood their trenches. Torrents would rush down the ranges and wash thousands of bodies out of their graves. The Anzacs had to break out now, while the weather was good.

Hamilton and Birdwood knew this. They also knew it would be easier to break out of Anzac than out of the British beachhead at Cape Helles. True, the British had advanced around 5 kilometres inland at Helles. But they still couldn't take that sullen-looking hill called Achi Baba. The stalemate was probably worse than at Anzac. There were no flanks that Lieutenant General Hunter-Weston, the commander at Helles, could work around.

Anyway, Hunter-Weston had shown himself to be a poor tactician. He really had only one tactic – the frontal attack in daylight. Hamilton had just about given up on frontal assaults by June, but he still allowed Hunter-Weston to waste more troops in useless charges. Hamilton was too polite to be a good commander. English teenagers sprang into their first day of battle and died in fields of wild flowers. Someone called the survivors the 'ghosts of Gallipoli'.

Hunter-Weston was a fox-hunting man whose manner was at once cheery and brutal. When a new division came out of its first battle with a frightful casualty list, Hunter-Weston said he was glad the 'pups had been blooded'. He kept running up casualties through June and July, when things were relatively quiet at Anzac. Corpses poked out of the Helles wheatfields, their fingers pointing to the sky.

Then Hunter-Weston suddenly left Gallipoli. Hamilton talked about him having a 'breakdown' but didn't say whether it was physical or mental. Hunter-Weston had been relieved of his command on the Western Front the previous year for reputedly 'going off his head'.

His 'pups' were as young as fifteen. Today, in Skew Bridge Cemetery, you can visit the grave of Drummer J. A. Townsend of the East Lancashire Regiment. He was the youngest Briton to die here. In a nearby Turkish cemetery lies Hasanoglu Ahmet, also fifteen years old when he died, and the youngest fallen Turk. We know little about him except that he was from Lapseki, in the Canakkale province.

Kitchener continued to refuse Hamilton the necessary supply of heavy guns, shells and hand grenades to even up the fight. To be fair, Kitchener wasn't getting the whole story. Hamilton sent messages brimming with optimism. He did not want to upset Kitchener, whom he called the 'demi-God'. He asked for more artillery, but his requests read like apologies.

Hamilton needed a win. British leaders did not properly understand the battles at Gallipoli, but they knew Hamilton was losing. So now his career virtually hinged on a plan Birdwood had been working on since May. Birdwood knew that he couldn't break out of Anzac with frontal charges. He suggested an advance from the northern flank of Anzac. It would take the shape of a great left hook.

Birdwood and his staff came up with the scheme after New Zealand scouts found a path through wild country to the unguarded Chunuk Bair. If the Allies captured Chunuk Bair, troops could stream back down Battleship Hill and Baby 700 and rout the Turks from behind. Reinforced with four brigades – 16 000 men – the Anzacs could take the third ridge of hills and march into Maidos.

Hamilton toyed with Birdwood's idea. Then London offered him an extra 60 000 men. He had to work them into Birdwood's plan. The chief virtue of Birdwood's original plan had been its simplicity. Now it would have to be expanded to include the fresh troops and a new landing north of Anzac. Things suddenly looked complicated.

It was decided that the Anzacs would launch three major attacks. On 6 August, the Australian 1st Brigade would charge the Turkish trenches at Lone Pine. This would distract the Turks from the attack on the heights. A similar feint would be carried out at Helles.

That night, while the battle raged at Lone Pine, Monash's brigade, alongside British, Indian and Gurkha troops, would scout untamed country to the north of the Anzac triangle, overrun Turk outposts in the foothills and take the highest point on the peninsula, Hill 971.

The orders were basic enough: trudge over and under and around a series of uncharted spurs radiating like fingers from Hill 971. Scale cliffs. Skirt ridges. And don't get lost.

New Zealanders would take Chunuk Bair, as in Birdwood's first plan. Hill 971 and Chunuk Bair were to be captured by dawn. At this time, the Australians would charge uphill at the enemy – from Russell's Top, the Nek, Pope's and Quinn's. The Turks would be fighting off Anzacs from above and below.

Meanwhile, at Suvla Bay, two fresh British divisions, about 20 000 men, would land, secure the surrounding hills, then try to link up with the Anzac position a few kilometres south. In his 5 August diary entry, Hamilton likened his pre-battle jitters to those of a patient about to undergo surgery. Failure would lead to fresh calls to evacuate Gallipoli. But Hamilton thought every possibility was covered. 'Nothing; not a nosebag nor a bicycle has been left to chance,' he wrote.

Hamilton hadn't thought about the terrain. The landscape north of Anzac is the roughest on the peninsula, a tangle of gullies and ravines, and waterless. The Anzacs who had to fight there were coming down with illness, mainly dysentery. The August offensive, as it would be called, was the biggest military operation at Gallipoli. Yet Hamilton, as always, was letting his heart rule his head.

CHAPTER ELEVEN

Of all the Bastard Places

6 August, Battle of Lone Pine

The battle of Lone Pine was the most stunning Australian success at Gallipoli. The main Turkish trenches were taken within half an hour. About 2200 Australians were killed or wounded in the Turkish trenches. The fighting was so savage that just about everyone who survived it was haunted for the rest of their lives.

The Anzacs threw bombs, some continuing even after a hand or an eye had been blown away, back and forth, with Turks only a few metres away. They thrust their bayonets at the enemy. They fought with their fists and feet. About 7000 Turks were killed or wounded. Seven Australians won a Victoria Cross and maybe a dozen more should have.

Brigadier General Harold Walker, the Australian 1st Division commander, was appalled by the plan. He didn't want his men wasted on a pointless charge over 100 metres of flat country. Walker admired his troops and they respected him, even if he was British brass. 'Absolutely buggered,' some had said, when he enquired after their health. Walker argued with Birdwood and won a few concessions.

Birdwood needed the Turks to treat the Lone Pine attack as a serious threat. Their reinforcements had to be kept from the heights. Walker plotted the charge carefully. A barrage of shells would destroy Turkish barbed-wire entanglements. Troops would then rush from the front-line, as well as from tunnels extending 28 to 37 metres out into no-man's-land. Other tunnels would be blown up to provide cover. The men would charge following a naval barrage at 5.30 pm on 6 August.

The veterans of the April landing were no longer happy adventurers. Grim self-respect drove them, wrote Bean, not a desire for glory. The newly arrived Anzacs were gung-ho. Some offered £5 bribes for front-line positions and fights broke out. Those to rush first wore white patches on their backs so that the warships did not fire on them.

5.30–6.00 pm

The Turks shelled the overcrowded Anzac lines just before the charge. Men dropped. The fumes were stifling. This is hell waiting here, thought Private Cecil McAnulty. Whistles blew in three short bursts. Two lines ran from the tunnel openings, two from the Anzac front-line trench. Palls of dust and yellow smoke hung in the sunlight. 'The fire was simply hellish, shell, rifle and machine-gun fire and I'm hanged if I know how we got across . . .' wrote a 2nd Battalion soldier. 'Every bush seemed to be literally ripped with bullets . . . our luck was right in.'

Few Anzacs were wounded in the charge itself. Many scrambled to the Turkish trenches, then halted, not knowing how to break in. Troops bunched up behind them. The Turkish trenches to the south were covered with pine logs. Some Anzacs found gaps in the roofing and jumped into the darkness below. It was in these trenches, in a clamour of shrieks and curses, that the battle of Lone Pine became a byword for hell. 'We was like a mob of ferrets in a rabbit hole,' said an Anzac, James Croker. 'It was one long grave, only some of us was still alive in it.'

Hundreds of one-on-one struggles broke out in the underground maze. According to one historian, Turks killed Turks and Australians killed Australians in the confusion. Bean wrote:

Many were killed within a few minutes of entering, since it was easy for a single Turk, at bay beyond a bend and warned by a bayonet coming around it, to shoot one man after another. In several places, Australians lay dead four or five deep . . . sometimes with a heap of Turks similarly killed a few yards distant from them.

The second and third waves of men stumbled over bodies. They tried to avoid treading on their faces. Private Jack Gammage leapt into the front trench and landed on a wounded Turk. 'We had no time to think of our wounded,' he wrote. '. . . their pleas for mercy were not heeded . . . some poor fellows lay for 30 hours waiting for help and many died still waiting'.

Some Turks ran away. A Turkish Battalion commander rushed down a gully yelling, 'We're lost! We're lost!' By 6 pm, the Australians held both flanks of the Turkish lines and seven or eight isolated outposts in between. Some outposts were no more than a few men and sandbags. Turkish reinforcements rushed forward with 'cricket ball' bombs.

The Australians threw jam-tin bombs. They smothered unexploded Turkish bombs with half-filled sandbags and anything else they could find. Many of the Turkish bombs were set to an eight-second fuse. They were lobbed back and forth up to three times until they exploded. 'For God's sake send bombs,' read a message from one of the outposts, just before it was engulfed.

Private McAnulty wrote about the charge a few days later:

I remember dropping down when we reached their trenches, looked around and saw Frank and three more men alongside me . . . I yelled out to the other four chaps, 'This is only suicide boys. I'm going to make a jump for it.' I thought they said all right we'll follow. I sprang to my feet in one jump . . .

McAnulty's entry finished there. Official records say he died between August 7 and 12. He was twenty-six.

7 August

Sergeant Cyril Lawrence worked in a Lone Pine communications trench on 7 August. He came across Australians crouched and wounded in a Turkish tunnel. They didn't say a word. Some had fallen asleep, including a man wounded in the head. Blood bubbled and frothed from his mouth. 'Yet all one gave him was simply a casual glance, more of curiosity than anything else,' Lawrence wrote. 'At ordinary times these sights would have turned one sick but now they have not the slightest effect.'

Lawrence gazed back at no-man's-land to see 'one mass of dead bodies, bags of bombs, bales of sandbags, rifles, shovels and all the hundred and one things that had to be rushed across to the enemy trenches'. Within five metres of him lay fourteen Anzac dead. 'Thank God that their loved ones cannot see them now,' he wrote.

Captain Ivor Margetts had been promoted since his brave charges on Baby 700 on the first day. He took over a section of a Lone Pine trench on 7 August. His men wore respirators to block out the deathly smell. The floor was spongy from lightly buried bodies. 'In the trench I counted 79653821650773982 flies who walked first on the perspiring live men and then, so as to cool their feet, they walked on the dead ones,' he wrote.

A month later Ion Idriess went up to Lone Pine. 'Of all the bastards of places this is the greatest bastard in the world,' he wrote. 'The roof of this dashed possy is intermixed with dead men who were chucked up on the parapet to give the living a chance from the bullets while the trench was being dug. What ho, for the Glories of War!'

9 August

The Australian VC winners at Lone Pine all fought in bombing contests. Two of them, Captain Alfred Shout and Corporal Alexander Burton, died of their wounds. Burton was hit by a bomb. He was said to smile quietly as he died. Shout, a New Zealand carpenter who lived in Sydney, ended up as the most decorated Anzac of the campaign. There's a photo of him at Gallipoli. He leans against the wall of a trench, all mischievous eyes and enquiring smile.

Shout fought in the opening-day battles at Baby 700. He carried a dozen men out of the firing line a few days later, despite being wounded, and earned a Military Cross. At Lone Pine, on 9 August, the day after his thirty-third birthday, he lit bombs and charged at Turks hidden around the next bend. He urged on his men all the way. Shout eventually lit three bombs at once. He threw one. One or both of the others exploded in his hand.

His hands were pulped. His left eye was blown out, his cheek gashed and his chest and one leg burnt. Yet his cheerful spirit was still intact. He sat up to drink tea as he was carted off to the beach. He assured all he would recover, but he died a few days later on a hospital ship.

Captain Frederick Tubb, Corporal William Dunstan and Burton fought a losing bomb exchange for hours on 9 August. There were ten men in their trench when the Turks counter-attacked. The Turks lobbed bombs and the Anzacs died one by one. Corporal F. Wright was killed when a bomb blew up in his face. Corporal H. Webb, an orphan, had both hands blown off when he tried to catch a bomb.

When five men were left, Tubb knelt on the parapet, in full view of the Turks, to fire his revolver. He was bleeding from his head and arm. When three men remained, a bomb exploded between them, killing Burton and blinding Dunstan. Tubb survived, to die in Belgium in 1917. It might be argued that all ten men should have received the highest honour. Corporal Webb received a Distinguished Conduct Medal. Corporal Wright received nothing.

William Dunstan was a reluctant hero. He was blind for almost twelve months afterwards. Pieces of shrapnel worked their way out of his body for years. His children had to tiptoe around the house because of his headaches. Sometimes their mother showed them the little bronze cross kept in the box underneath the stairs. When Dunstan died in 1957, aged sixty-two, he had never spoken a word to his children about 9 August 1915.

Lieutenant William Symons led a charge to retake a trench and fended off ferocious counter-attacks until the Turks gave up. Another Lone Pine VC winner, Private John Hamilton, was a nineteen-year-old butcher's boy from New South Wales. It is believed that he went on to three years of front-line service without being wounded. The VC also went to Lance Corporal Leonard Keysor, who was twenty-nine years old. He was born in London and returned there after the war. He later said that war was the only adventure he ever had.

Oliver Cumberland won neither medals nor fame. He had enlisted to protect his younger brother Joe, and now Joe was dead. Oliver had recovered from his leg wound to return to Gallipoli a few weeks before the August offensive. He wrote to his sister Una on 26 July:

> You can understand Una, that losing Joe has broken me up a bit, but Una it might be for the best – war is a terrible game, especially this war, and those who are killed quick are sometimes better off. I know it is useless to ask

you not to worry about me, but remember that I am used to roughing it and wars can end as suddenly as they start, and apart from the loss of poor Joe I am keeping my spirits up fairly well.

Oliver charged from one of the Lone Pine tunnels and dropped out of sight. The odds are he died trying to hold the most southerly outpost. Oliver likely became just another body in the way. Bean wrote of the outpost: 'The trench was literally floored with dead, in places several deep, and the fight, which was incessant, had to be carried on over their bodies.'

Back home, Una sewed children's clothes each night and fretted. Oliver's letters had stopped. She wrote to the Minister of Defence in October 1915, her tone deferential but desperate. Oliver's whereabouts was unknown, the military responded, but 'favourable progress may be assumed'. In December, Una received official word. Her brother was missing.

After the war, men masked in handkerchiefs poked the Gallipoli battlefields with rifle-cleaning rods. They stopped thrusting whenever the point plunged through disturbed soil. We can guess this was how Oliver's body was found, buried in an old trench near the present-day Lone Pine Cemetery. His identity disc, with sandy soil clinging to it, arrived in the mail at Kelly Street, Scone, in October 1922. Una finally had something to hold on to.

Oliver got more than most who died at Lone Pine – a

marked grave. Today, a lavender bush nestles alongside his headstone. Standing at the grave, you can see two pines bent and twisted by the breeze on the lonely swell of Baby 700. You can also see Chunuk Bair, which the Australians were supposed to take on 25 April. Perhaps Una chose the inscription:

> *A Brave Young Life That Promised Well*
> *At the Word Of God A Hero Fell*

25 April 2000

Surely the battleground was bigger than this? You can stroll from Brown's Dip, behind the Anzac lines, to the Cup, behind the Turkish line, in a few minutes. Dog-legged gutters, like old rabbit warrens, show where trenches were once dug in the prickly scrub.

Before Oliver's grave stands a white obelisk, near what was the front-line of Turkish trenches. It is the largest Australian memorial on the peninsula. On a long grey wall are the names of 3268 Australians who died at Gallipoli and have no known grave. Australians peer at the list, their eyes widening as they scan the names of young lives lost, and sigh.

The Lone Pine cemetery is bright with spring flowers. The wind howls as thousands of Australians and New Zealanders trek up here after the dawn service. Bodies lie amongst the graves. They are backpackers catching up on the sleep they missed the night before, wrapped in Collingwood jumpers and Wallabies guernseys.

Someone has placed a red rose next to Oliver's grave in the past twenty-four hours. John and Doreen Chick, from Martindale in the Hunter Valley, stand nearby. They are friends of the Cumberland family's descendants. And they are on a pilgrimage. They placed the rose on Oliver's grave. He hasn't been forgotten, after all.

The Lone Pine

Originally a single pine tree grew on the Lone Pine site, but it was whittled away by shellfire in the early battles. Australian soldiers called it 'Lonesome Pine', after a popular song of the time. They brought back cones from the tree to Australia. Thousands of pine trees now flourish in Australia, propagated from the Gallipoli cones. One tree raised from seed in Australia stands in the Lone Pine Cemetery at Gallipoli.

A 'lone pine' in the grounds of the Australian War Memorial, Canberra, was planted in 1934. It was given to the memorial, as a small tree, by the mother of a soldier killed in the battle of Lone Pine. His brother, who took part in the same attack, found a pine cone among the branches covering the Turkish trenches. From the seed, his mother raised the tree.

Sergeant Keith McDowell of the 24th Battalion carried home a pine cone and gave it to his aunt. Years later she raised four small trees, one of which was planted at the Shrine of Remembrance in Melbourne. Since 1965, Legacy has overseen the collection of seed and the propagation of 'lone pines'.

CHAPTER TWELVE

The Left Hook

Mustafa Kemal, the Turkish divisional commander, had been writing note after note to his superiors. The British would try to break out of Anzac, he told them. They would climb the hills to the north of Anzac. In July, Kemal's corps commander, Essad Pasha, finally granted him a hearing. The pair stood on Battleship Hill and stared at the mad country between Anzac and Suvla. Where would the enemy try to break out? Essad asked. Kemal waved his hand in a semi-circle, describing a big left hook. Essad looked at the cliffs and ravines. He smiled and patted Kemal on the shoulder. 'Don't worry,' Pasha said. 'He can't do it.'

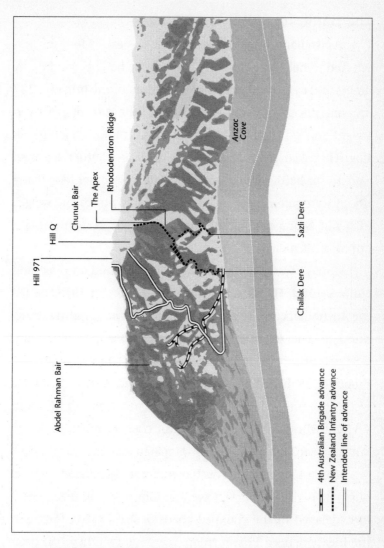

ROUTES PLANNED AND ROUTES TAKEN IN THE AUGUST OFFENSIVE

The Battle for Hill 971

The Australian 4th Brigade, under General Monash, was selected to help take Hill 971. The brigade had been cut up by illness and casualties. Nearly one hundred of the brigade's 137 original officers were out of action. At fifty years of age, overweight and worn down, Monash was unfit for such a difficult slog. He asked his four battalion doctors whether his men were fit for battle. Three said no. Apart from dysentery, many troops were suffering chest infections, rapid pulses and weight loss. But Monash felt that the excitement of battle might improve his men's condition.

Monash was a methodical planner. He had an open and curious mind. He liked new ideas. In France in 1918, he led the Australian corps to a series of victories and is rightly recognised as the finest general Australia has produced. But Gallipoli wasn't Monash's finest moment. On the night of 6 August 1915, he led his men into battle and ended up lost. He wasn't the only commander to falter. And it wasn't his fault. Anyone who has walked the bandit country north of Anzac knows it can befuddle the best-prepared visitor.

Monash's timetable was blown before his brigade started out that night. His troops were amongst a column of 5000 men delayed in the cramped chaos of Anzac Cove. Some of the inexperienced British troops were jumpy. They had been landed at night and hidden so the Turks would not detect troop build-ups. A few panicked soon after the column began trudging north along the beach. Bayonets were drawn to quell them.

Led by Major General Vaughan Cox, of the 29th Indian Brigade, the column turned right into the scrub towards Aghyl Dere, one of the mean little valleys twisting down from Hill 971. The rugged terrain meant that the route to Hill 971 was roughly the equivalent of 40 kilometres of flat country. A Greek guide suggested a short cut through a narrow pass. This was the first of many mistakes. Turkish snipers fired into the gorge. A shortcut to save thirty minutes cost several hours. And lives.

The moon rose and Turkish snipers began picking off Anzac troops as Monash led them into a field of olive trees, later to be named Australia Valley. Monash sent the 13th and 14th Battalions through the valley, and the 15th and 16th Battalions forward along Aghyl Dere. It appears that Monash had lost his bearings. It seems likely he was around 640 metres short of where he thought he was. Further up Aghyl Dere, the 15th and 16th came under Turkish fire and dug in. They, too, were not where they thought they were.

Dawn, 7 August

Cox arrived to speak with Monash. Monash argued against Cox's order to advance on Hill 971 at 11 am. Cox relented and allowed Monash to dig in. The Australians spent 7 August lying in holes scraped out of the ground, thirsty, wishing they were somewhere else. Gurkha and Indian troops wandered in the wilderness below Hill 971. They were not sure where they were meant to be. The column was scattered – like lost tribes, as one historian later put it – and unable to launch a meaningful assault.

Pre-dawn, 8 August

Three of Monash's battalions were ordered to advance on a spur known as Abdel Rahman – a ridge that led up to Hill 971 – before dawn. The Australians attacked lower outcrops, known as Hill 90 and Hill 100, thinking these were Abdel Rahman. Monash stayed behind and forfeited any chance of directing his men through the confusing terrain. As dawn broke, the Turks rained shells on Australians stranded in an oatfield. Four Turkish machine-guns helped cut down the Australian advance in under an hour. Some Australian wounded were left to die in the field. The stretcher-bearers had already left.

Private John 'Dad' Brotchie, of Melbourne, charged 275 metres through machine-gun fire. He was forty-four, and a father of nine. Brotchie bunkered down with a nervous soldier as shells burst overhead. 'He made me a nice cover and secured himself from harm by cuddling into me,' Brotchie wrote home. 'No room for arguments here but the bother was the shivers as each shell came over. I think I was right myself, but I could feel him shake and could pity him.'

The wounded of the 14th Battalion were carried back on stretchers made from rifles, coats and wood. Some hobbled. 'Poor helpless heart rending sights these,' Brotchie wrote.

> As we got round, the shells got us once more, hard and often, the men with wounded struggling up the hills and through the narrow gullies, gullies where a lean man could hardly squeeze through, and many a wounded man on a man's back got a nasty jar through these narrow sections.

The operation was a shambles. Even the retreat was bungled. Some troops never received the order to fall back. Thirteen Victorians, eleven of them wounded, were taken prisoner by Turks in tattered uniforms. Some of the men were bashed and stripped of their boots. The Turks looked set to throw the group over a cliff until German and Turkish officers intervened. Corporal George Kerr, twenty-three, had been shot in the arm and leg. An old Turk inspected his wounds and pulled out a big knife. The Turk walked to a tree, ripped off a branch and fashioned a walking stick for Kerr. Kerr survived the next three years as a prisoner-of-war on the Berlin–Baghdad railway.

The Australians were back where they started within a few hours. The 4th Brigade had suffered 765 casualties. In 1919, Bean trekked the slopes near Hill 100 and found skeletons in

14th Battalion colours. Explorers today can still turn up rusted ammunition clips and slivers of bone. The ragged landscape is mostly unchanged and unvisited.

Monash wrote a great deal after the war. He never clearly explained what went wrong in the attack on Hill 971.

The Battle for Chunuk Bair, 6–10 August

The New Zealanders sent to capture Chunuk Bair fared better. A New Zealand covering force cleared the foothills, including a small Turkish stronghold known as Old Number Three. For three weeks, a British destroyer had shined a spotlight on the position at 9 pm every night and shelled it for thirty minutes, sending the Turks underground. On the night of 6 August, the routine was replayed. This time, the covering force charged the Turkish trenches straight after the shelling. More than 100 Turks were killed.

Brigadier General Francis Johnston, commander of the New Zealand Infantry Brigade, led the right assaulting column that left Anzac at 11.30 pm, forty-five minutes late. Turkish troops on Table Top slowed his men when they clapped, cheered and surrendered. The column continued to Rhododendron Ridge, where they were to reunite with the Canterbury Battalion. But the Canterburys had lost themselves in a confusing valley. Many of them wound up back where they had started.

It was now 5.30 am, 7 August. The New Zealanders – three

in four of whom were said to be suffering dysentery – had shown great pluck. Colonel William Malone, the housekeeper of Quinn's Post, was at the Apex with his beloved Wellington Battalion. He was little more than 460 metres from the Chunuk Bair summit. About twenty Turks protected the peak. The Turkish commanders were caught out by the New Zealanders' advance, which had come at just the spot Kemal had predicted.

The Turks rushed reinforcements to Chunuk Bair. A German, Colonel Hans Kannengiesser, arrived at the peak ahead of his two Turkish regiments, at about 7 am. He spotted New Zealanders walking in single file below. He threw himself down and fired at them. On Johnston's orders, the New Zealanders took cover and ate a breakfast of bully beef and biscuits.

Johnston had just squandered the Allies' best chance of breaking out of the Gallipoli stalemate. He had disobeyed Birdwood's clear order to push on whatever the circumstances. The twenty Turks on Chunuk Bair would multiply into hundreds while Johnston waited below. Kannengiesser had time to gaze out over the salt lake to Suvla Bay. About 20 000 British troops were landing there, unopposed.

The Suvla landing went well, except for one hitch. The corps commander, Lieutenant General Sir Frederick Stopford, didn't order his men to advance strongly from the beach.

Stopford's appointment showed up the absurdities of the British class system. He had been plucked from retirement in England. He got the job only because of his seniority. He was sixty-one years old and elderly before his time. He had never commanded troops in battle before.

Stopford was probably the first commander to doze while his troops invaded a foreign shore. He didn't bother to send Hamilton a message until more than twelve hours after the first landings. His troops became intermixed on the beach. Many had been awake for seventeen hours before the landing. Orders were altered, cancelled, then reinstated. No one knew what they were supposed to be doing. Stopford slept on his ship and showed little interest.

When he awoke, Stopford told Hamilton that his men couldn't advance further than the beach. How he judged this is a mystery. Stopford didn't get to shore himself until forty hours after the first landings. The Turkish defences were light and scattered. Ever the kindly chap, Hamilton put up with Stopford's dilly-dallying. This was a bad misjudgment, but not Hamilton's worst. Suvla was always a sideshow to the struggles in the hills.

Brigadier General Johnston finally ordered his New Zealanders to attack Chunuk Bair at 10.30 am on 7 August. The near deserted peak of five hours earlier now bristled with Turkish machine gunners and riflemen. The Turks mowed down 300 Aucklanders as soon as they left the Apex. Johnston ordered Colonel William Malone's battalion to follow the Aucklanders. Malone refused. 'My men are not going to commit suicide,' he yelled at his superior. Johnston postponed the attack until the next morning.

Malone was prepared for death. In a loving letter to his wife, he apologised if he had neglected her for his business affairs. A lawyer, farmer and land agent, he suspected he had. His Wellingtons stood in lines of sixteen before dawn on 8 August. The crest was lit by the flames of an Anzac artillery barrage. The New Zealanders charged through the haze. British troops followed behind.

Given the New Zealand losses of the previous morning, Malone took Chunuk Bair with absurd ease. Only a few Turks had stayed through the artillery barrage. Malone's men took twenty as prisoners. The sun rose and Malone glimpsed what no Anzac had seen since 25 April – the Dardanelles. Capturing the peak had been easy. Holding on would be the awful part.

The New Zealanders were exposed to Turkish fire from nearby peaks. Snipers began picking them off after dawn. The hard, rocky ground held up the digging of trenches. The Turks could sneak to within 20 metres or so before they were spotted. They leapt into the shallow trenches with bayonets and bombs. The New Zealanders, like the Australians at Lone Pine, threw the bombs back.

Clouds of dust swirled in the stifling heat. Turks rushed forward. New Zealanders rushed forward. A front trench became so clogged with bodies that the New Zealanders stood on top of them. 'It's only when your tongue actually rattles round in your mouth that you can say you are thirsty,' a New Zealand private later said. 'That's no fable. Actually rattling around in your mouth. We stripped off to our tunics and we were fighting in singlets and in the buff'.

A bullet bent Malone's bayonet but he took this as a lucky omen. He went about urging his men on. A misguided Allied shell hit him late in the afternoon. Malone collapsed into an officer's arms and died. Sixty years later, a New Zealander who survived the battle still spoke fondly of 'Molly' Malone. He received no military decorations for his epic efforts on Chunuk Bair. Some say Malone should have won a Victoria Cross.

After dark, New Zealand reinforcements replaced the Wellingtons. Of the 760 Wellingtons who had advanced at first light, only forty-nine were unwounded. They staggered back, their torn uniforms drenched in blood. They had barely slept for two days. They had been thirsty since dawn. They trembled, whispered and cried. Casualties among the British assisting the Wellingtons had been nearly as heavy. Bolstered by reinforcements, the Turks had won back much of their side of the crest. Yet the Allies clung on.

By 9 August, the ill-advised Allied advances on Hill 971 had all petered out, bar one. About 450 British and Gurkha troops were poised to charge Hill Q, which lay between Hill 971 and Chunuk Bair. They lay hungry and thirsty in shallow dugouts below the crest as Turkish bullets thudded around them. The Gurkha 6th Battalion commander, Major Cecil Allanson, lay between two British soldiers. One read a Bible. At some point, Allanson realised the other was dead.

Allanson needed reinforcements, as did the New Zealanders on Chunuk Bair. Major General Alexander Godley was due to meet with senior officers to discuss these matters but he was waylaid by a phone call. He didn't bother sending a staff officer in his place. At the meeting, Johnston suggested that the 5000 British reinforcements approach Hill Q and Chunuk Bair from low ground. Had Godley bothered to survey the ground himself, he might have over-ruled Johnston's advice.

The British reinforcements hadn't slept for four nights. They blundered through dark ravines on the night of 8 August and got lost. They were nowhere near Hill Q or Chunuk Bair when the naval bombardment of Turkish trenches ended at 5.15 am. Turkish fire forced them to entrench at 6 am.

The Allied plans for 9 August were already scuttled. A co-ordinated advance on Chunuk Bair hinged on reinforcements and Johnston had sent them the wrong way. Allanson gave up waiting for extra men and charged Hill Q anyway. His men fought with their bayonets, fists and teeth. 'Blood was flying about like spray from a hair wash bottle,' he wrote. Allanson chased the Turks down the inland side of Hill Q until Allied shells began bursting among his men. They had been mistaken for Turks.

The New Zealanders on Chunuk Bair were trapped under renewed Turkish fire. They couldn't move. This fact didn't ruin an uplifting lunch for Hamilton, Birdwood and Godley at Anzac. The Allies had failed to reach any objectives, mainly because the planning had been botched. Yet the three men still believed they could reach the Dardanelles and that Chunuk Bair was safe in their possession. Holding on to Chunuk Bair remained the Allies' only chance of breaking through, but none of the commanders had bothered to properly monitor the battle there or look at the ground.

Kemal didn't issue orders from headquarters. He preferred to stand before his men and lecture them on martyrdom. Kemal schemed to get Chunuk Bair back. Unlike Birdwood and Godley, he realised that Chunuk Bair mattered more than any other position. Turkish officers suggested flanking movements to remove the Allied troops. The logical part of Kemal's mind tended to agree with this. But he was an instinctive leader. He decided on a frontal assault without the back-up of an artillery barrage. The enemy wouldn't expect that.

Kemal was gambling. He didn't know what or how many lurked on the other side of the hill. The charge had to be a surprise – otherwise his men would be wiped out by naval guns. Turkish losses had been heavy in the days before. A failed attack would open the way for an Allied push across the peninsula.

At dawn on 10 August, Kemal raised his riding whip. Thousands of shrieking Turks surged over Chunuk Bair. Young British volunteers had replaced the New Zealanders on the crest the night before. They heard the rumble before they saw the bayonets. Some were swept away before they knew it. Others stumbled down the steep slopes to the valley floor some 180 metres below. New Zealand machine-gunners fired on the Turks, as did the navy. But it all happened so fast. Chunuk Bair was lost in a few minutes.

A group of British troops was stranded for two weeks near the valley floor. They drank from a spring and scrounged food from the dead. Turks came across them and refused to take them prisoner. The British began to starve. Most of them rushed together down the valley to escape. It appears that Light Horsemen mistook them for Turks and fired on them. Those who rushed were never seen alive again. The seven who stayed behind were rescued by New Zealanders.

Kemal still frowns down on the peninsula from Chunuk Bair. Busloads of New Zealand tourists stare up at his bronze statue. Chunuk Bair to them is much like Lone Pine is to Australians. The statue commemorates Kemal's lucky escape. During the charge of 10 August, his pocket watch was said to have stopped a piece of shrapnel from piercing his chest.

Kemal had been right about the Allied plans to break the stalemate. After the August offensive, he took to his July diary notes with red ink. He wrote in the margins that those who had dismissed his theory about the 'left hook' had been 'mentally unprepared'. They had endangered the nation, he wrote.

Gallipoli made Kemal. After the Great War, he led Turkey to victories over the Greek invaders in 1922. As Atatürk, he became Turkey's first president and set about wrenching his nation into the twentieth century. He was ashamed of what he saw as his country's backward ways, as compared to those of western nations. He set about turning Turkey into a secular republic. He was as ruthless a politician as he was a soldier, and he ranks as one of the great reforming figures of his century.

CHAPTER THIRTEEN

Murder at Dawn

The Battle for the Nek, 7 August

Kemal was a good general and got better as the Gallipoli campaign went on. He was nothing like Ian Hamilton. He enjoyed responsibility. He was always a realist. He had a ruthless streak, and it showed in his hard eyes. He could quickly reduce a problem to its essentials. But he still made mistakes. One of those was to order a charge from the Turkish trenches at the Nek on 30 June. The Turks suffered 800 casualties to the Anzacs' twenty-six. The dead and wounded Turks in no-man's-land reminded an Australian sergeant of poisoned rabbits.

The conclusion was simple. Frontal charges at Anzac didn't work. Kemal learnt his lesson and didn't order another.

The Allied commanders learnt more slowly. As part of the August offensive, Australians on Russell's Top were ordered to charge the Nek at dawn on 7 August. The charge was supposed to slot into the bigger scheme. The New Zealanders, as we know, planned on capturing Chunuk Bair by dawn. They would stream down the heights to attack the Turks from behind. The Australians at the Nek would charge up the hill as the New Zealanders charged down.

As we know, the New Zealanders got held up. Their commander, Brigadier General Johnston, lingered below the crest of Chunuk Bair. His decision condemned 600 Australians to charge at Turkish trenches without support from higher up the ridge. Yet we can't blame Johnston for what happened at the Nek. Lieutenant General Birdwood knew that the New Zealanders had been delayed. He also knew about the failed Turkish charge of 30 June. He could have called the Australian charge off. Yet we can't just blame Birdwood either. Or his subordinate, Godley.

The truth is that the Australian commanders on the spot could have cancelled the charge at the Nek. They chose not to. Two regiments of the 3rd Light Horse Brigade ran at Turkish machine-guns with bombs and bayonets. They leapt from the trenches and crumpled like rag dolls. They died for nothing.

The Light Horsemen at Russell's Top relished the promise of battle. They were bored after eleven weeks of carting water and digging trenches. They were tired of dust and flies. Some imagined the upcoming charge as an escape into open country. Wasn't it bad enough that they'd given up their horses to foot-slog like plain infantry? Those with wounds and illnesses begged their doctors to allow them back to the front-line. They knew the charge would be risky but they didn't want to miss out.

The 8th and 10th Regiments of the 3rd Light Horse Brigade would run with the sun in their eyes. The Turkish trenches opposite lay eight-deep. The first wave of Light Horsemen would take the first trench, the second the rear trenches. The third wave would chase the enemy – it was assumed the Turks would retreat – while a fourth would drag shovels to entrench their gains. Each Anzac was to carry 200 rounds of ammunition, a field dressing kit, a full water bottle and two empty sandbags.

The Nek was a thin strip of dusty ground leading up the range from Russell's Top. There were steep drops on either side. The Nek narrowed like a funnel. It was only about 25 to 35 metres wide at the Turkish trenches. Only 150 men could charge in each wave. Two Turkish machine-guns sat opposite the Australian trenches and at least two others sat on the flanks. Each machine-gun could fire about 500 bullets a minute.

The brigade's commander, Brigadier General Frederick Hughes, was opposed to the charge at first, as was his subordinate, Lieutenant Colonel John Antill. Hughes, fifty-seven, had risen through the citizen soldier ranks, the equivalent of today's Army Reserve. He delighted in marching drills and crisp saluting. At Gallipoli, his first war, Hughes was too old and too inexperienced. He delegated much of his authority to Antill, a Boer War veteran nicknamed 'Bullant' by the troops. The two met with Godley when the August offensive was being planned. There is no evidence that either argued strongly against the plan.

Pre-dawn, 7 August

The Light Horsemen shivered in shirts before dawn on 7 August. The nights had been chilly, but a fussy clerk had ordered the troops to hand in their greatcoats. The soldiers were given two tots of rum at 3 am. David McGarvie, the crack shot with the cleft palate, who had battled to sign up for war, didn't have the time or peace-of-mind to sleep.

The bombardment boomed louder than any had for weeks. Then it stopped – seven minutes early. So much for the element of surprise. (It is suspected that watches had been incorrectly synchronised.) Silence fell as the first line of Anzac troops gathered. Everyone knew the plan had already gone wrong. The Turkish machine-gunners rattled off a few practice rounds.

Lieutenant General William Birdwood swims in the Aegean. (AWM G00401)

Colonel John Monash survived Gallipoli to become Australia's most famous military leader.
(AWM A01241)

General Sir Ian Hamilton the day after he was sacked as Allied commander-in-chief.
(AWM H10350)

The youngest Anzac, Private James Martin, before leaving for war.
He died in October 1915, aged fourteen.
(AWM P00069.001)

Lieutenant Hugo Throssell in a London hospital after earning the Victoria Cross at Hill 60.
(AWM P00516.003)

Taking aim with a periscope rifle.
(AWM A04045)

Captain Alfred Shout was the most decorated Anzac at Gallipoli. He died after the battle of Lone Pine, where he earned the Victoria Cross.   (AWM G01028)

Making bombs out of jam tins, explosives, shrapnel and barbed wire.
(AWM G00267)

A blindfolded Turkish envoy is carried over wire entanglements by naked Anzacs. (AWM G00988)

Australians and Turks bury fallen soldiers during the truce. (AWM H03954)

A self-firing rifle devised to give troops time to evacuate without the Turks noticing. (AWM G01291)

Dragging a water tank up the hills above Anzac Cove. (AWM G01117)

The wounded below Pope's Hill on the morning of 7 August.
(AWM C02707)

An officer mourns the loss of a mate.   (AWM G00419)

Chaplain Ernest Merrington uses biscuit boxes and a scrap of cloth as an altar. (AWM P01875.004)

Anzacs playing cricket on Shell Green to distract the Turks from the evacuation. Shells can be seen exploding in the background.
(AWM G01289)

An unidentified Anzac in France. The 'A' on his shoulder denotes service at Gallipoli. (AWM E03886)

Bayonets bobbed in the Turkish trenches. The Turks knew what was coming.

The commander of the 8th Regiment, Lieutenant Colonel Alexander White, looked down at his watch. White could have stayed behind but he felt a duty to lead the charge. Personal belongings such as books and keepsakes sat in piles. White had kept the locket carrying a photo of his wife and young son around his neck. 'Go,' he yelled, and the first wave bounded forward.

The journalist Charles Bean was nearby. The Turkish machine-guns exploded in 'one continuous roaring tempest'. God help anyone that was in that tornado, Bean thought. The Turkish trenches were between 35 and 80 metres away. Most Australians fell within a few metres of the Anzac parapet. Some pitched backwards into the trench. An observer said that the men fell to the ground 'as though their limbs had become string'. White ran about ten paces and died. His men were wiped out in thirty seconds.

Sergeant Cliff Pinnock felt a 'million ton hammer' fall on his shoulder within 10 metres of the Australian trench. His mates fell around him like lumps of meat. A bullet had entered Pinnock's shoulder and come out near his spine. 'Well, we all got over and cheered, but they were waiting ready for us and simply gave us a solid wall of lead,' he wrote from hospital.

McGarvie tripped over barbed wire. His rifle, helmet and

haversack, with his Bible, bounced off in different directions. He picked himself up, raced through a 'hail of bullets', and dived into a gully a few metres from the Turkish trenches.

'The only thing I could see worth shooting at was a Turk bayonet, two yards in front, so I fired and snapped it clean in two,' he wrote to his parents. 'Then the second row of Turks stood up showing heads and shoulders. I got some splendid shots; altogether I fired about 10 shots, and I am certain of four or five Turks. Then I felt a terrible crack on the foot.'

McGarvie's letter is rare evidence to suggest that at least a few Turks were wounded in the attack. No Anzac officers survived the first wave. Most of them were dead in seconds. Turkish bullets continued to thump into the bodies as the wounded scrambled for cover. The Nek stunk of cordite and death.

Pinnock crawled back to the Anzac trenches. He grieved for his mates. They'd spent every hour of every day together for months. Later, he 'cried like a child'. 'There was no chance whatever of us gaining our point, but the roll call after was the saddest, just fancy only 47 answered their names out of close on 550 men,' he wrote.

The second wave charged two minutes later. Like the first, it was wiped out in thirty seconds. McGarvie, lying in no-man's-land, turned his head to watch. 'They just mowed them down, and hardly a man reached the trench,' he later recorded. '. . . I saw dozens of wounded turn back and make for our trench, but never got more than a few yards, so I made up my mind to stay there till dark.'

It seems unlikely that any Anzacs reached the Turkish trenches, although an observer reported seeing an Allied red-and-yellow marker flag in a Turkish trench. Trooper Vernon Boynton came close. 'I got within about six yards of their trench when I seemed to be hit everywhere through my right leg, my right forearm, my right hand, the first finger of which was hanging off and blood pouring everywhere,' he wrote to his sister.

Most of the second wave were added to the growing pile of bodies near the lip of the Anzac trenches. The scrub quivered with Turkish fire. One soldier, Trooper White, fell unconscious, with four dead Australians on top of him. In less than three minutes, nearly four in five men in the 8th Regiment had been killed or wounded. Not an inch of ground had been taken.

The 10th Light Horse stepped over and around bodies in the Anzac trenches as Turkish shells began bursting over no-man's-land. Surely the 10th wouldn't be sent over? There was nothing to be gained and everything to be lost. The 10th Regiment's commanding officer, Lieutenant Colonel Noel Brazier, peered through a periscope at the carnage. He couldn't order his men to die.

Brazier rushed back to brigade headquarters to ask Brigadier General Hughes to call the charge off. Hughes was elsewhere, observing the second wave. Instead, Brazier spoke with Antill. The two men had never got on. Antill told his subordinate that a flag had been seen in the Turkish trenches and that the attack must continue. Brazier argued that the flag sighting was most unlikely. Antill didn't bother to consult Hughes. According to Brazier, he simply roared: 'Push on.'

Brazier returned to his troops and said: 'I am sorry lads but the order is to go.' Seven officers shook hands and said goodbye to one another. Trooper Harold Rush, a farmhand, turned to his mate and said: 'Goodbye cobber. God bless you.'

The third wave rushed at 4.45 am to 'meet death instantly'. Among them was Wilfred Harper, a farmer, who was seen 'running forward like a schoolboy in a foot race'. Harper's dash was part of the inspiration for Peter Weir's moving film, *Gallipoli*. The film depicts a British officer sending waves of Anzacs to their certain death. In truth, Anzacs sent Anzacs to their certain death.

Major Tom Todd lay in no-man's-land, pinned down under Turkish fire. He scribbled a note asking for further orders. Brazier presented the note to Antill, who once again told him to push on. Brazier returned to the front trench and received another note from a stranded officer. Brazier now bypassed Antill. He wanted Hughes' instructions on what should happen to the fourth wave.

Major Joe Scott, commanding the line, awaited Brazier's return. Then another tragedy struck. It appears that men on the right of the line mistook an officer's wave as an order to charge. Many men leapt forward before Scott could stop them.

The third and fourth lines suffered fewer casualties than the first two. Many sensibly rushed for the nearest cover. Lieutenant Hugo Throssell liked to crack jokes. He urged his men to a small hollow, then announced: 'A bob in, and the winner shouts.'

'At first here and there a man raised his arm to the sky, or tried to drink from his waterbottle,' Bean wrote. 'But as the sun of that burning day climbed higher, such movement ceased. Over the whole summit the figures lay still in the quivering heat.'

McGarvie lay stranded for more than fifteen hours. His feet lay across a Turk who had probably died in the 30 June assault. The slightest movement invited Turkish bullets, but he fired at nearby Turks anyway. He lay near a fallen soldier whose leg was hooked up in the scrub. The Turks fired at the dangling leg until it dropped down.

McGarvie moved after dark. He couldn't stand, so he dragged himself like a worm for about 275 metres. He called out when he was near the Anzac trenches. A sentry fired at him. Perhaps for the first time ever, McGarvie felt blessed for his cleft palate. Another trooper with a cleft palate also had an unusually muffled voice. McGarvie was mistaken for him and told to get in fast. He died in 1979, aged 86.

The 8th Regiment sent out 300 men and suffered 234 casualties, including 150 dead. The 10th had 138 casualties, including eighty dead. At least four sets of brothers died at the Nek. So too did a Rhodes scholar.

Australians tried to hook ropes around the corpses in no-man's-land, to drag them in for burial. One man was found to have been clasping a prayer book when he died. But most of the dead rotted where they fell. In 1919, an Australian mission counted more than 300 Australian bodies in an area no larger than three tennis courts. In the Nek cemetery, no one knows who lies where.

The high command didn't much talk about what had happened at the Nek. Ian Hamilton didn't mention the charge in his war diaries. Godley gave it one sentence in his autobiography. The survivors didn't talk about it either, although some nicknamed the strip of land 'Godley's abattoir'.

The charge at the Nek is considered the saddest waste of Australian lives at Gallipoli. William Cameron, a 9th Regiment sergeant who watched the charges, said the troops fell like corn before a scythe. 'Yes, it was heroic, it was marvellous, the way those men rose, yet it was murder,' he wrote.

CHAPTER FOURTEEN

The Last Stand

Suvla, Hill 60 – Late August

The August offensive failed mainly because Hamilton and his commanders didn't do their homework. They tried to blast their way out of their Anzac fortress without checking the escape routes. The confusing hills and gullies conspired to defeat the Allied troops as much as the Turks did. Hamilton's plan had not allowed for a single hold-up. Yet the mad terrain had caused many.

Nor did it help that Birdwood and Godley ran their battles from headquarters. They issued orders about battles they barely understood because they weren't on the ground. Both made reckless assumptions and ignored simple truths.

The volunteer soldiers had been let down by their career commanders. Lone Pine had been the only victory – and it was a diversion. The Turks would never surrender Chunuk Bair. Hill 971 had never been seriously threatened. The Turks at the Nek celebrated their victory and wondered if the Anzacs would be silly enough to try again. After four days, the Allies had taken no territory that mattered, despite 12 500 Anzac casualties. The British officer Aubrey Herbert summed up the position: 'On the hills we are the eyebrows and the Turks are the forehead.'

The campaign looked to be lost. Hamilton, as usual, refused to acknowledge the obvious. 'Birdie [Birdwood] and Godley are at work upon a scheme for [Chunuk Bair's] recapture,' he wrote in his diary. 'The Turks are well commanded: that I admit. Their Generals knew they were done unless they could quickly knock us off our Chunuk Bair. So they have done it. Never mind: never say die.'

Hamilton's last hope rested with Lieutenant General Stopford and the Suvla landing. Stopford had conjured reasons to keep his troops on the beach. He spent the days after the landing thinking up more fanciful excuses.

Hamilton's patience ran out after Stopford explained that his troops could not attack because the Turks were 'inclined to be aggressive'. Stopford was sacked on 15 August. He slinked back to London and filed the military equivalent of an unfair dismissal claim.

By then, Suvla had become another hopeless siege. The surrounding hills were relatively clear when Stopford's men landed. But the Turks had occupied the high ground as Stopford stalled and fussed for forty-eight hours. The British troops at Suvla lacked experience and basic supplies. The *Daily Telegraph* journalist Ellis Ashmead-Bartlett found patches of scorched khaki where 'another mismanaged soldier of the King had returned to mother earth'. A company of King George's farmhands charged into smoke and disappeared.

Hamilton wrote a lengthy report to Kitchener. He admitted the offensive had failed and asked for more troops. He also urged his commanders to take extra ground. Maybe he thought that a lot of small wins might make up for several huge losses.

Birdwood wrote to his wife that his Anzacs were as 'weak as cats'.

Two furious battles on 21 August were hardly worth dying for. The Allies wanted to secure the Suvla beachhead and join the Allied line from Suvla to Anzac Cove. But winning these battles wouldn't put the Allies any closer to the Dardanelles. Many Australians died in savage struggles on Hill 60, a small rise about halfway between Anzac and Suvla.

The British staged a bigger battle at Scimitar Hill, a few kilometres inland from Suvla. The hill erupted in smoke and flames. British reinforcements fell like tenpins on the dry salt lake as Turkish shrapnel shells burst above them. Wounded men were burnt to death in scrub fires. By nightfall, British casualties stood at 5300 out of 14 300 men. No ground had been gained.

The Australian attack on Hill 60 started the same afternoon and lasted for more than a week. Monash's brigade was down to 1400 men, compared with 4000 when he landed. His men rushed at Hill 60 in charges almost as suicidal as those at the Nek.

Two lines of 150 Anzacs went forward through wheatfields and thick scrub, carrying picks, shovels and barbed wire. The Turkish trenches had been undamaged by an earlier bombardment. The first Anzac wave went in and 110 men fell. It was much the same with the second line. Bushfires broke out and 'Dad' Brotchie, of the 14th Battalion, watched 'writhing bodies trying to get away from the fire, the ammunition from the pouches going off and exploding'. Chaplain Andrew Gillison was shot dead trying to rescue the wounded. He was buried wrapped in a Union Jack. Chaplain E. N. Merrington removed Gillison's wedding ring and sent it home to his wife.

The 18th Battalion, from New South Wales, had been ashore three days when it was ordered to Hill 60. The old Anzacs looked like scarecrows. The new men looked fresh and clean. They were told to charge the Turkish trenches at Hill 60 with bayonets and bombs, even though they had no bombs.

About a quarter of the 750 who charged were killed in their first battle.

Private Myles O'Reilly disobeyed orders and loaded his rifle before the charge. He was squeamish about the thought of bayoneting a Turk. He helped take a Turkish trench when the enemy ran away. Turks started throwing bombs from O'Reilly's left. He climbed onto the parapet to fire when a bomb exploded behind him. O'Reilly was badly wounded but lived. He always suspected that the hard biscuits in the haversack on his back saved his life.

Private James Grieve, of the 18th Battalion, survived the first charge and battled Turks for the next thirty-five hours. In a letter to his parents, he wrote of bullets and shrapnel whizzing around his head. The smell of piled dead bodies was 'awful but that was not the worst'.

> We were in such a cramped position & it was almost
> impossible to get water & I never felt the want of water so
> much in my life before. I would have given all I possessed
> in this world to have had a real good drink of water.

Grieve signed off the letter with a row of fifteen kisses. It was found in a dugout near Hill 60 on the same day that he was killed.

The remnants of the 10th Light Horse regiment rushed Hill 60 on 28 August and took Turkish trenches. Lieutenant Hugo Throssell, a 31-year-old farmer, had been in the fourth wave at the Nek, three weeks earlier. Now he piled sandbags to stem Turks rushing from around trench corners. He shot five men before the Turks began lobbing bombs.

The Australians threw their own bombs. As at Lone Pine, unexploded bombs went back and forth in trenches less than 10 metres apart. Anzac rifles burned so hot, they had to be swapped for those of the dead and wounded. Throssell held the trench, despite being shot in the neck and shoulder. Beside him was Corporal Syd Ferrier, a Victorian in his mid-thirties. Ferrier kept throwing bombs even after a Turkish bomb burst in his hand and blew away his arm to the elbow. He walked away for treatment but died on a hospital ship.

Birdwood thought Hill 60 had been taken. Yet the Turks still held half the summit. The Allies had suffered 2500 casualties without gaining control of the hill. The Australian 4th Brigade was down to under 1000 men. 'The whole was a rotten, badly organised show – and those who planned it are responsible for heavy loss to this brigade,' Monash wrote in his diary.

Throssell's shirt was peppered with bomb fragments when he left the line. His wounds stiffened so that he could not hold a cigarette to his mouth. He returned after having his wounds dressed but a superior officer ordered him to leave and not come back. For his actions on 29 August, Throssell became the last Australian VC winner at Gallipoli.

CHAPTER FIFTEEN

Intrigues

Some British politicians resented Hamilton's campaign even before he left England. They believed that the Dardanelles scheme stole troops and weapons from more critical battles in France. The campaign was supposed to have been swift and decisive. Now, after the failure of the August offensive, it had become an embarrassment.

Hamilton's leadership had been questioned for months. The journalist Ellis Ashmead-Bartlett had returned home in June, mainly to replace clothes lost when his boat was torpedoed, but also to express his concerns to Prime Minister Herbert Asquith, and to Churchill, Kitchener and other power-brokers. Ashmead-Bartlett had doubted the campaign

tactics from the start. His habit of explaining his ideas to anyone who would listen had infuriated Hamilton's staff.

By August, some of Hamilton's own staff had lost faith in
him, much as they admired him as a man. They knew he fed
Kitchener reports that were absurdly optimistic. One of the
staff officers, Guy Dawnay, was chosen to go to London.
Dawnay was well connected. He spoke to King George – who
had lost faith in Hamilton – and to everyone else who mattered. Dawnay had set himself an impossible task. He tried to
remain loyal to Hamilton while explaining that the
Dardanelles campaign was failing.

His mission was muddled by intrigues in London. The war
cabinet fumbled with the difficulties of a world war it had not
yet begun to understand. No war had ever been this vast.
Bulgaria was now edging towards joining forces with Germany,
which would allow Germany to transport heavy guns to
Gallipoli. With more guns, the Turks might blow the Allies off
the peninsula. Some politicians wanted to stay at Gallipoli.
Others fretted that a loss would cripple British prestige.

Then Keith Murdoch, an Australian journalist, arrived in
London from Gallipoli. Murdoch had prospered as a reporter
in Australia after earlier failing to entrench himself in
London's Fleet Street press. He had overcome a stammer that
sometimes left him unable to speak. At thirty years of age,
Murdoch was patriotic and quick to judge. He also knew how
to manipulate people. He said openly that he wanted to be a

'power'. He thought more about courting politicians than improving his writing, which was often windy. Myth has it that Murdoch wrote a letter that prompted the British government to evacuate Gallipoli. The truth is more complicated.

Murdoch was approached in 1915 to set up a cable service in London for Australian newspapers. He stopped in Egypt to do a minor job for the Australian government. For a fee of £25, he was to investigate delays in the Anzacs' mail service. He went to Gallipoli, met Hamilton, and wandered around the peninsula for a few days. He also met Ashmead-Bartlett, and fell under his spell.

Ashmead-Bartlett's criticisms of the campaign inspired Murdoch to breach the British government's censorship regulations. He would take a damning letter, written by Ashmead-Bartlett, to the British Prime Minister. Murdoch was stopped by military police when he left his ship in France and forced to surrender the letter. Hamilton had been tipped off about it, probably by another journalist outraged at the breach of censorship rules. Murdoch travelled on to London and wrote his own letter, intended for the Australian Prime Minister, Andrew Fisher.

Murdoch's letter, dated 25 September, made similar points to Ashmead-Bartlett's, but his tone was scornful, his attitude know-it-all. Murdoch got facts wrong. He had

Gurkhas fighting on Hill 971. He falsely stated that British officers were directed to shoot soldiers who lagged behind. His troop and casualty numbers were wrong. Murdoch was smitten by the Anzacs, and wrote that the British soldiers at Suvla lacked endurance and brains.

The errors didn't matter much. Important politicians wanted the Gallipoli campaign to end. This letter helped their cause. And for all its faults, Murdoch's statement captured the hopelessness of Gallipoli. He pointed out that the medical arrangements were scandalous. Naval guns of low trajectory, he wrote, were useless when opposing trenches were metres apart. Murdoch wrote that the Anzac trenches would slide away when winter set in. He had, of course, obtained much of this information from Ashmead-Bartlett.

A London newspaper editor introduced Murdoch to senior British politicians opposed to the Dardanelles campaign. One suggested that Murdoch send his letter to the British Prime Minister. Asquith printed the document as a state paper and distributed it. Murdoch had finally become a man of influence. Others, however, deserve more credit for ending Gallipoli.

Dawnay was in London, explaining the critical situation, ten days before Murdoch got there. Ashmead-Bartlett had been sent home when his original letter was intercepted. He did what Murdoch didn't do – he created headlines. He gave a newspaper interview outlining his concerns. His criticisms were reported in the Australian newspapers.

Australia's new Prime Minister, Billy Hughes, was asked in federal parliament what he thought of Ashmead-Bartlett's opinion. 'I do not pretend to understand the situation but I do know what the duty of this government is, and it is to mind our own business, to provide our quota of men for the Imperial Government, and to see that they are efficiently led, fed and equipped,' Hughes said.

Australia still considered itself an outpost of the British Empire in 1915. Hughes' parliamentary colleagues were said to loudly cheer his statement.

They had encouraged their brightest and fittest countrymen to enlist in a foreign war. Thousands of Australians lay dead on the other side of the world. And the war was none of their business?

October

Kitchener wrote to Hamilton about 'unofficial reports' criticising the Dardanelles staff for being out of touch with the troops. Kitchener suggested that Hamilton replace some of his staff. Bound by old-fashioned loyalty, Hamilton refused. In doing so, he probably gave up any chance of saving his own job.

The Dardanelles Committee in London asked Hamilton's opinion on likely casualties if the peninsula was evacuated. Hamilton was shocked by the suggestion. He replied that half of all men and supplies would be lost.

At a meeting on 14 October, two committee members argued strongly that Gallipoli should be evacuated. The committee also decided that Hamilton should be replaced. Kitchener was directed to break the news. Hamilton was woken late at night to be told there was a message for his eyes only. He went back to sleep. He guessed that he had been sacked. He would read about it in the morning.

Hamilton's superiors had never given him enough men or artillery to take the Dardanelles. But Hamilton had never put his case strongly enough. He was too soft, both with London and his own troops. He was the wrong man in the wrong place, and had been from the start. Hamilton's ship weaved through the anchored vessels as he left Gallipoli on 17 October. The general stood on deck. Sailors stood and cheered as he passed.

CHAPTER SIXTEEN

The Barometer Swings

September–November

Many Anzacs who landed at Gallipoli in or after September never saw a Turk. The August offensive was the last great military battle of the peninsula war. Shells and bombs still fell out of the sky. Rifle-bursts still echoed across no-man's-land. But now there were moments of silence. Both Turks and Anzacs had grown weary. The troops continued to fight, but mostly against nature.

The Anzacs grumbled about the poor showing of the British at Suvla. They were tired of fatigue duties and slimy bully beef. Australian Sergeant Cyril Lawrence came across Anzacs gambling in a trench. The betting revolved around the direction a beetle would take when released from a jam tin.

'You'd say it was childish, harmless lunacy, and yet here, this ability of the happy-go-lucky colonial to amuse himself and delight in childish amusements, has been all that has kept him sane,' he wrote.

About 200 Anzacs were evacuated with illness every day. Sticking it out on the peninsula was considered a point of honour. Take the Anzac who reported to a doctor in September with 'a little trouble'. He had dysentery, a badly broken arm and two bullet wounds in his thigh. Another bullet had passed through his diaphragm and liver before exiting his body. The private had been first wounded on 25 April.

Many of the new arrivals succumbed to illness. James Martin, from Melbourne, arrived with the 21st Battalion in September. He spent six weeks at Gallipoli, alternating between front-line duties and fatigues. 'It is quiet where we are so we are not seeing much of the fun,' he wrote in October.

Martin's scrawled letters home spoke of the squalor endured by both Anzacs and Turks. 'There was one Turk who tried to give himself up the other night and got shot by the sentry,' Martin wrote. 'We dragged him into our trenches to bury him in the morning and you ought to have seen the state he was in. He had no boots on, an old pair of trousers all patched and an old coat.'

Family history has it that Martin forced his parents to sign an enlistment consent form. He threatened to run away to war and never write if they refused. Martin finished his final letter from Gallipoli by begging his mother and father to write. Letters from home had not reached him since he left Victoria nearly four months earlier.

Martin died of heart failure on a hospital ship after contracting enteric fever. His official papers said he was eighteen. But James Martin was fourteen years and nine months old. He was the youngest Anzac to serve at Gallipoli. His possessions were sent home. They included a red and white streamer he had picked up when his troopship left Melbourne.

The Southland

Thirty-two Australians died on 2 September 1915 when the transport ship *Southland* was torpedoed, near Lemnos Island. Those on deck saw the approaching torpedoes but could do nothing. One torpedo blew a large hole in the side of the ship on the waterline, while a second passed harmlessly by. Within hours nearby ships had rescued most of the troops, and a team of volunteers stayed on the *Southland* and successfully stoked the crippled ship into port.

The Turks suffered the same miseries as the Anzacs. Official figures state that more than 20 000 died of disease on the peninsula. A Turkish officer's diary, published in 1997 as *Bloody Ridge*, shows that the Turks were just as worn out as their enemy. They shied from shells and questioned their leaders. They longed for letters from home.

Mehmed Fasih was a 21-year-old lieutenant in the Turkish trenches at Lone Pine. He had been wounded in May but returned to the front in October. War had turned his hair and beard grey. He was itchy from lice and fleas. Fasih read novels out loud with fellow officers, smoked a pipe, listened to rumours and feared death.

Anzac shells blew up sections of the Turkish trenches almost daily. Fasih described six bodies after a shell hit a machine-gun emplacement. 'Blood has drained out of bodies, and chests and arms look like wax,' he wrote. 'Shins and legs, seared by the explosion, are purple. Some bones have been stripped of flesh. The men's features are unrecognisable.'

Fasih was taken to see the mutilated body of a friend. The sergeant's head and chest were ripped open. His eyes stared at the sky. Warm tears washed down Fasih's face as he helped bury his friend under an olive tree. 'I can't stand it anymore,' he wrote in his diary. 'What sorrow! . . . Have already witnessed so many deaths and tragedies. But none affected me to this extent. As a matter of fact, very few upset me anymore.'

By November, Fasih's face was wrinkled and his skin was rotting. Turkish troops prodded with bayonets refused to attack and started 'crying like women'. Fasih was convinced he would die at Gallipoli. 'Will I ever have a child who will call me "Daddy"? Please, God, allow me to live to see that day . . . !'

Fasih had heard rumours that the Allies would leave. He and fellow officers wondered about the long lulls in enemy firing. Were they foxing or were they leaving?

First came hail, then rain, then sleet, then snow. Lightning lit up the horizon. The Aegean Sea reared black and frothy. Dugouts flooded. Lips turned blue and toes turned black. Wind whistled through the trenches and the Anzacs understood why trees didn't grow tall at Gallipoli. The winter storms – that's why. One man died of exposure at Anzac while dozens of British and Turks froze to death. At Suvla, British soldiers drowned in flooded trenches. In late November, the Turks lobbed a note into the Anzac trenches at Lone Pine. 'We can't advance,' the note read, 'you can't advance. What are you going to do?'

Hamilton's replacement, General Sir Charles Monro, believed the war would be won or lost in France. He toured the Gallipoli trenches and asked a few questions. Commanders told him that their troops could launch a 24-hour offensive. But they didn't know whether troops could survive the winter. That was all Monro needed to know. He recommended an evacuation.

Kitchener schemed to save the campaign. But the politicians had woken up to him. The Gallipoli debacle had begun to expose him as less than a 'demi-god', and probably not fit to be running the war. Kitchener arrived at Anzac Cove on 13 November, wielding a walking stick. Bedraggled Anzac troops rushed to cheer him to shore. His was probably the most famous face in the British Empire.

Kitchener was shocked when he saw the crazy landscape. No wonder his troops hadn't taken the Dardanelles. He toyed with alternatives but he had none. Winter was coming and the Allies would be washed off the peninsula. Kitchener reluctantly recommended an evacuation. London dilly-dallied, as usual. Finally, it was decided. Gallipoli had been a mistake. It was time to go.

CHAPTER SEVENTEEN

Farewell to the Fallen

December

Escaping Gallipoli was going to be just as dangerous as invading it. The challenge was to remove 80 000 men, 5000 animals, 2000 vehicles and 200 guns from Anzac and Suvla. If the Turks found out, tens of thousands of Allied troops could be slaughtered on the beaches.

The soldiers would leave over a number of nights. Boats would creep in, load men, and disappear. Before the dawn mists lifted, the beach had to look the same as it had on the previous day. The Turks needed only to break through at one Anzac point to expose the deception. And we know from Mehmed Fasih's diary that they suspected something was up.

Allied command estimated losses of between 20 and 50 per cent during evacuation, which would equate to at least 16 000 men being killed or captured. The plan was kept from the Anzac troops. Senior commanders feared that the Turks might hear the news. In some places the trenches were so close that the Turks could hear the Anzacs talking. But no orders could stop gossip. Few Anzacs swallowed the official line that troops were being thinned for the winter period.

Some Anzacs relished a potential end to bad food and raging disease. But others now considered Anzac their property, the muddy holes their homes. They had staked their territory and their mates had died defending it. 'If it were true! God!' wrote Cyril Lawrence of the rumours on 10 December. 'I believe that murder and riots would break loose amongst our boys . . . Oh, it couldn't be; how could we leave this place now after the months of toil and slavery that have gone to the making of it?'

Monash described the news as 'stupendous and paralysing'. There was talk of disobeying orders to stay in the trenches. The 2nd Brigade was said to beg for one final 'go' at breaking the stalemate. Lawrence felt ashamed. 'Better to struggle and die fighting our way ahead than to sneak off like a thief in the night,' he wrote.

The evacuation was better planned than any Allied attacks at Gallipoli. Monash issued each 4th Brigade soldier with a card detailing his task, time of departure and route to the beach. Trails marked by salt or flour would guide the men to the beach. The last to leave were to pull across barbed wire behind them.

Tricks were staged to suggest that all was normal. Those silent periods that Fasih wondered about in November? They were 'silent stunts', aimed at getting the Turks used to lulls. Most medical staff left early, but their tents remained on the beach. Men were ordered to loaf around and smoke where Turks could see them. On the afternoon of 17 December, Light Horsemen played cricket on Shell Green. A famous photo depicts a soldier belting a front-foot drive while three shrapnel shells burst in the background.

All went well at first. Men and supplies and mules left each night. Some Anzacs may have grumbled but they co-operated with their orders. At least they'd enjoyed decent food, wine and clothing from the stores opened up on the beach. The weather stayed calm and the Turks tried no surprises. On the last two nights, only 20 000 men defended Anzac. Now for the tricky part.

The front-line trenches were the last to be evacuated. Trench floors were ploughed or laid with blankets to silence footfalls. Lance Corporal W. C. Scurry, of the 7th Battalion, invented a self-firing rifle to give departing soldiers a head start. A kerosene tin was punctured so that it dripped water into a tin below. After about twenty minutes the lower tin over-balanced, tripping a piece of twine that triggered the rifle to fire.

After dark on 18 December, half the remaining men left on a smooth sea. The situation grew more tense. If the Turks attacked now, they would break through. Men tidied the graves of their mates and bade them farewell. An Australian nodded towards a cemetery and told Birdwood: 'I hope *they* won't hear us marching back to the beach.' Some smashed what they couldn't take, so that the Turks couldn't use anything.

One soldier set a table for four, with jam, bully beef, bis-cuits, cheese and tobacco. He left a note. 'There are no booby traps in this dugout', he wrote. This was not quite true. He had opened some rifle shells, poured out the black gun pow-der, and mixed it into the packets of ready-rubbed tobacco. Another soldier left a note telling the Turks, 'You didn't push us off, Jacko, we just left.'

By 11 pm on 19 December, less than 2000 men held the entire Anzac line. Sergeant Cliff Pinnock had survived the Nek charges on 7 August. Now he was among the last to leave Gallipoli. Pinnock was set to leave the front-line for the beach in a few hours. The moon shone and the temper-ature dropped. Pinnock's feet froze. He didn't think twenty pairs of socks could warm them. 'The last day was simply awful,' he wrote. 'I never in all my life want to go through such another day.'

Pinnock had been instructed not to fire unless he was certain he saw a Turk. The problem was that he thought he saw Turks everywhere. 'My God, I would have given anything in the world to have been able to open up and let go a hundred or so rounds just to ease my nerves,' he wrote. 'At 12 o'clock I was in that state that I dared not look at any object for more than a few seconds, if so I could clearly imagine I saw a man rise and place his rifle to his shoulder.'

At 2.15 am, Pinnock was ordered to march the 4 kilometres to the waiting boats. There had been 36 000 Anzacs here a few weeks earlier. Now there were a few hundred. Some were so exhausted from the nervous strain that they had to be prodded to stay awake. No one spoke as Pinnock's group trudged to the beach. The men had rigged rifles to fire when trench candles burned down. As they walked, they heard the guns going off. The Turks opposite returned fire.

Men from the 24th Battalion stayed at Lone Pine until the end. The last group was about to leave, at 2.40 am, when an officer found a man on the parapet taking 'just one more pot at them'. The officer heard explosions and found an Australian throwing the new Mills bombs. 'It's a pity not to use them,' the Anzac said. 'They're great.' An officer thought he saw two Turks emerging from a tunnel, until one man said: 'A bonzer night. It'll be a pity to leave the old joint.'

Pinnock clambered into a boat that moved off for Lemnos

as spent bullets plopped into the sea all around. A few hours later, he bribed a ship steward and had his first bath in months. He soaped off his lice and threw his stinking clothes out the porthole.

The last boat left Anzac at 4.10 am. Private F. Pollack, of the 13th Battalion, was nearly left behind. He awoke in a dugout to find the area deserted. He raced to the beach. It was deserted. He rushed to North Beach and caught one of the last boats.

Underground explosions, set off at 3.30 am, killed seventy Turks at the Nek, and prompted Turkish fire right across the line. The Turks did not discover the evacuation until after dawn. Only two men were wounded in the Anzac evacuation, including one hit in the arm by a spent bullet as he left the beach. At Suvla, and later Helles, there were virtually no casualties.

Almost every major event had got away from the Allied commanders since 25 April. Only in the leaving of Gallipoli could they claim a triumph. Monash watched from a ship as the Nek exploded like a volcano of dust. He felt that the evacuation was 'a most brilliant conception, brilliantly organised, and brilliantly executed – and will, I am sure, rank as the greatest joke in the whole range of military history.'

Casualties

Casualty numbers include those killed, wounded, missing, sick or taken prisoner. About one million men, from both sides, were involved in the Gallipoli campaign. Between 50 000 and 60 000 Australians served on the Peninsula. About 64 000 Australian cases of sickness were reported, and seventy Australians were taken prisoner.

Below are the numbers of dead and wounded at Gallipoli.

Country	Died	Wounded	Total
AUSTRALIA	8709	19 441	28 150
NEW ZEALAND	2701	4852	7553
BRITAIN	21 255	52 230	73 485
FRANCE (est)	10 000	17 000	27 000
INDIA	1358	3421	4779
TOTAL ALLIES	44 023	96 944	140 967
TURKEY	c.86 000	c.128 000	213 882

CHAPTER EIGHTEEN

Judgment

The Gallipoli legend bloomed in Australia before the Anzacs left the Turkish peninsula. Heroes had been anointed and a few villains cast. The heroes were ordinary men who had done extraordinary things. Blokes like John Simpson and Albert Jacka and the bomb-throwers from Lone Pine and Hill 60. Australians accepted that their first major campaign had ended in military defeat. But this wasn't the point. Gallipoli was a triumph of the Australian spirit. The Australians had hung on. Gallipoli was about mateship and fatalism and rough humour. Gallipoli had honour. It gave a new nation a sense of the worth of its people. Nearly nine decades on, this judgment still holds up.

The cast of villains has changed over the years. Winston

Churchill was promptly blamed, in both England and Australia, for much of the failure of the Dardanelles campaign. It was said that his soaring vision had clouded older and wiser minds. Churchill went on to bigger things. His belligerent faith steered Britain through desperate times in World War Two. Australia was never high in Churchill's priorities. When Singapore fell in 1942 and Australia looked vulnerable to Japanese invasion, Churchill did little to help. He travelled extensively over his lifetime but never visited Australia.

The Australian troops of 1915 blamed the British volunteers who landed at Suvla for the failure of the August offensive. This is not entirely fair. The inexperienced troops were asked to do too much. They were also badly led.

The reputations of the Gallipoli generals took a long time to crumble, but crumble they did. One cannot blame them for failing to understand the new warfare of the industrial age, with its reliance on artillery rather than horses and bayonets. But one can blame generals such as Hunter-Weston and Godley for being arrogant and careless.

And Ian Hamilton? It is fair to say that his temperament was wrong for a command like the Dardanelles campaign. Gallipoli destroyed Hamilton's career but not his spirit. Hamilton opened war memorials and wrote books until his death, aged ninety-four, in 1947. Hamilton stayed true to character until the end. He never blamed Kitchener or others for the Gallipoli failure.

Kitchener escaped public roastings – but only because he drowned in 1916, when his ship struck a mine on the way to Russia.

William Birdwood commanded the Anzacs until 1918. He was so fond of Australians that he hoped to become Australia's governor-general in the 1930s. He missed out when Australia, in a sign of growing maturity, decided that an Australian should finally have the posting.

Harold Walker, the best-liked British general at Gallipoli, commanded an Australian division until 1918, despite being badly wounded at Gallipoli in October 1915. John Monash went on to become Australia's most famous military commander. He led 150 000 Anzacs to victories in France in 1918. Monash died in 1931, aged sixty-six, and 250 000 turned out on Melbourne streets for his funeral. Godley and Hunter-Weston both went on to command corps in France.

So quickly did the Gallipoli legend grow that Australian politicians and newspapers in 1916 opposed a British government inquiry into the Dardanelles campaign. There was a fear that the facts would damage the legend. The inquiry's findings in 1919 were predictable enough. Kitchener had taken on too much work and been too secretive. Hamilton hadn't given Kitchener enough information during the campaign. The Turks' strengths had been under-estimated, and the plans for the August offensive had been impractical.

Journalist Charles Bean followed the Anzacs to France and Belgium, then devoted his life to writing the official Australian history of the Great War. It makes for heavy reading but Bean's knowledge of the detail of battles was unmatched. Always humble, he refused a knighthood.

One Woman at Gallipoli

Only one British woman is believed to have landed at Gallipoli. To this day the true circumstances of her visit are steeped in mystery. On 17 November 1915 the woman came ashore at V Beach, and laid a wreath at the lone grave of Lieutenant Colonel Charles Doughty-Wylie, VC, who had been killed at that spot on 26 April.

Doughty-Wylie was an intelligence officer on Sir Ian Hamilton's staff. He was awarded the Victoria Cross posthumously, for leading a successful attack.

One report says that the woman spoke to no one. She may have been Doughty-Wylie's wife, Lillian, who was nursing in France. But she may have been Gertrude Bell, the English writer and explorer, who was Doughty-Wylie's lover.

Perhaps Turkish women visited troops at Gallipoli. But their story is yet to be told.

The Gallipoli legend is so ingrained that separating facts from myths can be difficult. We all learn about the Anzacs when growing up. We are taught that Simpson was brave and that the British got it wrong. Both statements are true enough, but the most powerful tales of Gallipoli are about men you don't often hear about any more. Alfred Shout and Bill Dunstan throwing bombs at Lone Pine. Alexander White leading the charge at the Nek. Jack Gammage overcoming his nerves and Oliver Cumberland grieving for his brother.

Sometimes we bathe Gallipoli in a romantic glow. We talk about the Anzac spirit and mateship and good humour. The Australians at Gallipoli had all these qualities. But they also had dysentery and toothaches to think about. They stank of dirt and death and wondered whether they could go on. They crawled out of holes to dig more holes, fetch water, or if they were lucky, take a quick dip before the next shrapnel storm. They dreamed of a bath or a piece of steak.

Lieutenant Colonel Alexander White didn't come home from Gallipoli. He bubbled with enthusiasm when he enlisted. 'Dear little wife and kiddie,' he wrote, not long before dying in the first wave at the Nek. 'I seem so far away from you all; I do not want to speak about the war; it's horrible. If I let myself think too much about it my nerves would go. Have seen things and done things I want to forget.'

Many of the Anzacs came home and couldn't forget. Yet they couldn't talk about Gallipoli either. Lieutenant Hugo 'Jim'

Throssell, who won a VC at Hill 60, was never the same. He had been renowned for being the first with the funny line when he landed at Gallipoli. He changed when his brother died in battle, in 1917. Throssell shot himself dead in 1933. In his will, he wrote: 'I have never recovered from my 1914–18 experiences.'

Many Australians think Gallipoli was solely an Anzac war. This wasn't so. Some 8700 Australians died on the peninsula. About one million men on the two sides served at Gallipoli, and between one third and one half were killed or wounded. More than 86 000 Turks died. The British lost 21 255 men, the French lost 10 000, and 2701 New Zealanders died.

For decades no one much visited the Gallipoli cemeteries. In 1984, about 300 people attended the 25 April dawn service at Ari Burnu, and many of them were Gallipoli veterans returning for the first time. Some thought Anzac Day would fade away. Then something happened that no one can easily explain. Young people wanted to find out more about Gallipoli. Teenagers began asking about their great-great uncle's death at Lone Pine. Perhaps the distance of time softened the grisly truths of Gallipoli. Young people cast their imaginations back to 1915 and marvelled at how different Australians were then. How reckless they were. How generous. Gallipoli is now a destination for Australian pilgrims, most of them young people.

The last surviving Gallipoli veterans were honoured as 'living monuments' in the 1990s. Alec Campbell received more media attention when he died in 2002 than a former prime minister who died soon afterwards. Campbell spent less than six weeks at Gallipoli and saw no major fighting. This didn't matter. His death severed our last link with the legend. Campbell had lied about his age, gone to Gallipoli, and then lived to be 103 years old. This made him a grand figure, whether he chose to be or not.

Pre-dawn, 25 April 2000

Up to 15 000 Australians have rugged up against the Aegean Sea breeze. They are here for the Gallipoli dawn service. Young people drink slabs of beer before the dignitaries arrive. They break out into 'Advance Australia Fair' and wonder if they will stay awake. A long day of larking stretches ahead. Once they've paid their respects, of course.

Gentle waves flop onto the pebbly shore. In another world, eighty-five years ago, Simpson and countless others landed on this beach, north of Ari Burnu. Back then, manhood was measured on the battlefield. Australians called themselves British. Now Turkey welcomes the annual 'invasion' of Australians. 'Hello Anzac,' yell the street traders and rug merchants of Istanbul.

Few Australians gathered here could explain the folly of

the August offensive. Some don't even bother to poke around the hills and valleys where the Gallipoli legend was made. A pebble or a handful of sand will do as a memento. Maybe a photo of Simpson's grave. Then it's back to the bus. But Gallipoli is forgiving like that. You don't have to wrestle with the detail to feel its pull.

Just before dawn the ridges behind North Beach show up like arthritic fingers. Politicians take turns in trying to express what Gallipoli means. But you keep turning back to the cliffs. Wind and rain have eroded them but they still look out over everything. It's what the Anzacs saw rise out of the blackness when they landed on 25 April 1915.

How would we face battle? This is what the Australian battalion commander Walter McNicoll wondered as his men climbed into the boats. The Australians did well in their debut, as many saw it, on the world stage. Later, they did even better – in France and Belgium. Nearly six times as many Australians died there than died at Gallipoli. Cliff Pinnock, the nervous evacuee, died in France. So did Ivor Margetts, the Hobart school teacher who fretted that the Gallipoli landing would make or mar the name of Australia.

Monash, too, sensed that Australian deeds at Gallipoli would linger in history. 'I suppose that some day, on some high plateau overlooking Anzac Beach, there will be a noble memorial erected by the people of Australia, to honour the memory of their fallen dead, who lie peacefully sleeping in the little cemeteries in the valleys around,' he wrote during the campaign.

There are memorials all over Gallipoli now, soaring white columns, thousands upon thousands of headstones, a lost generation mouldering in the tawny ground of a foreign field. But these memorials are perhaps not as affecting as sitting alone in the dark on the Gallipoli shore and letting your imagination take hold.

As the blackness turns to an inky blue, you think you can glimpse the lifeboats and see the faces of young men from Adelaide and Hobart. Grim faces of men going to war, men going out to kill other men. And innocent faces, too, wide-eyed and open. Because on that April morning these young Australians had no notion of how terrible war could be.

They are all gone now, these men. And in another sense, because they have found their way into our hearts and minds, they are with us forever.

Appendix I – Soldiers Write Home

Oliver Cumberland writes to his sister.

Cairo

31-5-15

Dear Una,

I suppose you received my last letter in which I told you I was slightly wounded. I am quite well now and expect to go back to the front any time, but Una, prepare yourself to hear the worst if you have not already heard it – poor Joe is gone – he died of wounds in Alexandria hospital on the fifth of May. I did not know until yesterday, I went to headquarters offices in Cairo and saw the list of killed and wounded. I had been very anxious wondering where he was, and when I saw the list I did not know what to do. I wandered about the streets nearly mad, I felt so lonely. I am letting you know at once because I think it is always best to know the truth, however sad. He died for his Country Una, I know how you will feel sister – God help you all to bear it.

If I can get away for a couple of hours when I pass through Alexandria, on my way back to the front, I will visit the hospital where he died and see if he left any message.

I received a bunch of letters from home yesterday and two

postcards from Doris. I suppose you will have seen the list of killed and wounded in the papers before you get this.

I think the worst of the fighting in Turkey is over now, it could not be any worse than it was the first few days.

Well dear sister there is no more to say so I will conclude, with best love to all

Your affectionate Brother
Oliver
My address is still the same.

Colonel William Malone, writing from Anzac to his two young sons, 9 May 1915: it must have taken some effort to find something cheerful to write about.

I see lots of strange things here, big ships and little ones, aeroplanes and all sorts of guns and things. Soldiers and sailors. The other day a tortoise called on me. There were two or three of them living in a bank close to where I slept. I lived on the bank too. There were lots of frogs. I didn't see them, but they made such funny croaking – not like our frogs. Something like birds with a bad cold.

A letter from Private John Simpson:

28.2.15

Dear Mother,
Just a line to let you know that we are leaving Egypt today. I don't
know where we are bound for but hope that it will be England or
France. Now Mother you will have to excuse short note as we are all
in a hustle and bustle to get the transports waggons [sic] *packed*
and leave this afternoon. So with love to you and Annie

I remain
Your loving son
Jack

A letter home from Private James Grieve.

Firing Line
Aug 27th 1915

Dear Mum and Dad,
Just a few lines to let you know that I am still alive and doing fairly well
under the circumstances. After leaving Heliopolis where I wrote the last
letter from, we went to Alexandria in the train, and there we boarded
the boat. We didn't see much of Alexandria as we got right off the
train and on to the boat. We left Alexandria on the 16th of August on

the Alunia *and had a very good trip as far as the island of Lemnos. It took us two days to come from Alexandria to Lemnos, and it was a beautiful trip, and I think I would have enjoyed it only that I had a bad attack of toothache and I had to have it pulled out and the Dr. nearly pulled my head off. We stayed at Lemnos for a day, but we didn't get off the boat. We were transhipped off the* Alunia *on to a smaller boat the* Partridge *and we left Lemnos at about 6 o'clock on Thursday afternoon on the 19th and arrived at the Dardanelles at about midnight the same night. It took us till nearly daylight to unload our Battalion and all our gear and ammunition, and it was the hardest bit of work I have done since I joined the army. After landing we went up into a bit of a gully where it was a bit safe, and although bullets and shells were whizzing over our heads I had a good sleep. That night Friday we moved to another quarter and made ourselves comfortable in a dug out and camped there till Sunday morning. At two o'clock on Sunday morning we were all roused out of bed and told that we had to make a charge. We had to march over a mile to the place and not knowing the country it took us longer than it should have, and we didn't get into the charge till daylight and the result was that a good number of our boys were bowled right out and also a good number wounded. We lost both our captains, one was wounded and the other killed, also one Lieutenant was killed out of our company. It was awful to hear the moans and groans of the wounded and dying. One poor chap lying a few feet away from me was wounded in the knee. I bandaged it up for him as well as possible and he started to crawl back but I heard after that he was shot dead while crawling back 'poor fellow'. There were bullets and machine guns whizzing all around, also shrapnel which is worst of all. It fell all around me and several chaps fell around me and yet I escaped. It was marvellous how I came out without a scratch, but I expect it was my luck. After the charge, I got into a trench which about 60 of our Batt. were in and there we had to stop for about 35 hours and keep the Turks at bay. In that trench things were awful. Our own dead, and also dead Turks lying all around and the smell was awful but that was not the worst. We were in such a cramped position and it was almost impossible to get water and I never felt the want of water as much in my life before. I would have given all I possessed in this world to have had a real good drink of water. But we hung out and it was a great relief to get out of it. I never wish to have the same experience again. Since coming out of the trench we have only been sapping and digging trenches and although we are always in a more or less dangerous position it isn't too bad. Well Mum and all at home I hope this little note finds you all well and that you will not think I am forgetful for not writing sooner but I can assure you this is the first opportunity I have had since I landed here and I will write at every available opportunity. Remember me to all at Kellyville and tell Ag to give my best love to all the girls down at the Palace, also to Mary F. I will now close with love to all at home from your ever loving son James.*

Jim.

A. Sparrow sends his best love to Sis. Also does M. T. C. Butler.
xxxxxxxxxxxxxxx

Appendix II – Australian VC Winners at Gallipoli

The Victoria Cross is the highest award for bravery in the British armed forces. The medal was instituted by Queen Victoria in 1856. Thirty-nine Victoria Crosses were won during the Gallipoli campaign, nine to Australians.

The Victoria Cross is made of bronze, which was cast from the metal of guns captured from the Russians during the Crimean War.

Australian recipients of the VC at Gallipoli are:

Lance Corporal Albert Jacka (14th Battalion), at Courtney's Post, 19–20 May 1915

Lance Corporal Leonard Keysor (1st Battalion) at Lone Pine, 7–8 August 1915

Lieutenant William Symons (7th Battalion) at Lone Pine, 8–9 August 1915

Corporal Alexander Burton (7th Battalion) at Lone Pine, 9 August 1915

Corporal William Dunstan (7th Battalion) at Lone Pine, 9 August 1915

Private John Hamilton (3rd Battalion) at Lone Pine, 9 August 1915

Captain Alfred Shout (1st Battalion) at Lone Pine, 9 August 1915

Lieutenant Frederick Tubb (7th Battalion) at Lone Pine, 9 August 1915

Lieutenant Hugo Throssell (10th Light Horse Regiment) at Hill 60, 29–30 August 1915

Select Bibliography

Books

Australian War Memorial, *Guide to the Battlefields, Cemeteries and Memorials of the Gallipoli Peninsula*, Third Edition, 2002.

Ashmead-Bartlett, Ellis, *The Uncensored Dardanelles*, Hutchinson, 1928

Aspinall-Oglander, Cecil, *Military Operations: Gallipoli*, two volumes, Heinemann, 1929, 1932.

Bassett, Jan, *Guns and Brooches*, Oxford University Press, 1992.

Bean, Charles, *Official History of Australia in the War of 1914–1918*, Volumes I and II, Angus & Robertson, 1940; and *Gallipoli Mission*, ABC Books, 1990.

Blainey, Geoffrey, *Eye on Australia*, Schwartz and Wilkinson, 1991.

Bowers, Peter, *Anzacs*, Australia Post, 1999.

Burness, Peter, *The Nek*, Kangaroo Press, 1996.

Butler, A. G., *Official History of the Australian Army Medical Services 1914–18*, Volume I, Australian War Memorial, 1938.

Carlyon, Les, *Gallipoli*, Macmillan, 2001

Cochrane, Peter, *Simpson and the Donkey*, Melbourne University Press, 1992.

Davies, Harry, *Allanson of the 6th*, Square One Publications, 1991.

Denton, Kit, *Gallipoli: One Long Grave*, Time Life Books, 1986.

East, Ronald (ed), *The Gallipoli Diary of Sergeant Lawrence*, Melbourne University Press, 1983.

Facey, A. B., *A Fortunate Life*, Penguin Books, 1981.

Fasih, Mehmed, *Lone Pine (Bloody Ridge) Diary of Lt Mehmed Fasih*, Denizler Kitabevi, 2001.

Fewster, Kevin (ed), *Gallipoli Correspondent*, Allen & Unwin, 1983.

Gammage, Bill, *The Broken Years*, Penguin, 1975.

Godley, General Sir Alexander, *Life of an Irish Soldier*, E. P. Dutton, 1939.

Hamilton, Ian, *Gallipoli Diary*, two volumes, George H. Doran Co, 1920.

Harvey, Sergeant W. J., *The Red and White Diamond: Official History of the 24th Battalion AIF*, McCubbin, 1920.

Herbert, Aubrey, *Mons, Anzac and Kut*, Arnold, 1919.

Hill, Anthony, *Soldier Boy: The True Story of Jim Martin*, Penguin, 2001.

Idriess, Ion, *The Desert Column*, Angus & Robertson, 1932.

James, Robert Rhodes, *Gallipoli*, Pimlico, 1999.

Kerr, Greg, *Lost Anzacs*, Oxford University Press, 1997.

Mackenzie, Compton, *Gallipoli Memories*, Cassell & Co, 1929.

Macdougall, Tony, editor, *War Letters of General Monash*,
   Duffy and Snellgrove, 2002.

McMullin, Ross, *Pompey Elliott*, Scribe Publications, 2002.

McNicoll, Ronald, *Walter Ramsay McNicoll 1877–1947*,
   privately published biography.

Murray, Joseph, *Gallipoli As I Saw It*, William Kimber, 1965.

Pederson, Peter, *Monash as Military Commander*, Melbourne
   University Press, 1992.

Phillips, Jock; Boyack, Nicholas; and Malone, E. P., *The Great
   Adventure*, Allen & Unwin, 1988.

Pugsley, Christopher, *Gallipoli: The New Zealand Story*,
   Hodder & Stoughton, 1984.

Robson, L. L., *The First A.I.F. A Study of its Recruitment
   1914–1918*, Melbourne University Press, 1970.

Robertson, John, *Anzac and Empire*, Hamlyn Australia, 1990.

Schuler, Phillip, *Australia in Arms*, T. Fisher Unwin, 1916.

Scott, Ernest, *Official History of Australia in the War of
   1914–18*, Volume XI, Angus & Robertson, 1936.

Shadbolt, Maurice, *Voices of Gallipoli*, David Ling Publishing,
   2001.

Snelling, Stephen, *VCs of the First World War: Gallipoli*,
   Sutton Publishing, 1999.

The Anzac Book, Cassell & Co, 1916.

Wanliss, Newton, *The History of the Fourteenth Battalion AIF*,
   The Arrow Printery, 1929.

Articles

The *Age*, Melbourne, issues from August 1914 to December 1915.

Anonymous, 'Discipline', *The Duckboard*, 1 November 1924.

Anonymous, 'How The VC Is Made', *The Duckboard*, 1 March 1921.

Argus, Melbourne, issues from August–December 1915.

Brotchie, Phil, 'A Soldier's View of War: Grandfather at Gallipoli', the *Genealogist*, September 1996.

Dix, Charles, 'Efficient Navy: How Troops Were Landed', *Reveille*, March 1932.

Dunstan, Keith, 'Unsung Hero's Number Comes Up', *Bulletin*, 30 April 1996.

Hamilton, Ian, 'Lack of Guns In Gallipoli Campaign', *Reveille*, September 1932.

Robertson, J. C., 'The Landing: Epic Feat', *Reveille*, 31 March 1931.

Tame, Adrian, 'The Greatest Love Of All', *Sunday Herald-Sun*, 19 May 2002.

Tate, Brian, 'The Assassin Of Gallipoli', *Courier-Mail*, 24 April 1993.

Diaries and Letters

The following are all to be found in the collections of the Australian War Memorial, Canberra.

Private Arthur Blackburn	AWM 2DRL/0650
Private Joe Cumberland	AWM PR86/147
Private Oliver Cumberland	AWM PR86/147
Private J. K. Gammage	AWM PR82/003
Private James Grieve	AWM PR91/079
Private Cecil McAnulty	AWM 1DRL/0422
Captain Ivor Margetts	AWM 1DRL/0478
Private James Martin	AWM PR85/339
Chaplain E. N. Merrington	AWM 1DRL/0496
Sergeant Cliff Pinnock	AWM 1DRL/0547
Private John Simpson (Kirkpatrick)	AWM 3DRL/3424

Private Letters

Colonel Walter Cass (courtesy of Diana Cousens)
Private David McGarvie (courtesy of Christine Gascoyne)
Private Myles O'Reilly (courtesy of Tom O'Reilly)
Lance Corporal Phil Robin (courtesy of Robin Ashwin)

Websites

Australian War Memorial:	awm.gov.com.au
Visit Gallipoli at	anzacsite.gov.au
Visit the Imperial War Museum at	iwm.org.uk/

Film and Video

Australians at War (episode 2), Beyond Productions, 2001,
ABC documentary series.

Forgotten Men: The Human Experience of World War I,
Canal+Images International, 1999. Originally made in
1934 from footage at the Imperial War Museum.

Gallipoli, feature film directed by Peter Weir, 1981.

Gallipoli: History in the Depths, Turkish documentary, English
translation by SBS Australia.

Gallipoli: The Fatal Shore, reported by Chris Masters for
the ABC.

Gallipoli: The Last Crusade, Ed Skelding Productions, 1999.

Gallipoli 1915: The Bloody Peninsula, Castle Communications
PLC.

Great Military Blunders, Channel Four Television Corporation,
UK.

Heroes of Gallipoli, Australian War Memorial. Ellis
Ashmead-Bartlett's movie film from Gallipoli, with titles
by Charles Bean.

Kitchener: The Empire's Flawed Hero, a Brook Lapping
Production for the BBC.

The Anzac Legend, Interface Production and Direct Video,
1990.

Endnotes

Chapter One

'Why don't the – fire', quoted in Bill Gammage, *The Broken Years*,
    page 54

'Tell the colonel that the damn fools', quoted in Charles Bean,
    Official History of Australia in the War of 1914-18, Vol I, page 252

'Look at that', quoted in Charles Bean, page 252

'Klock-klock-klock, wee-wee-wee', quoted in Gammage, page 55

'With a sharp moan or low gurgling cry', Charles Bean, page 254

'Just like little birds', quoted in Charles Bean, page 254

Story of Donald and Arthur Veitch from Adrian Tame, *Sunday
    Herald Sun*, 19 May 2002

'Then began the strain of waiting' quoted in Ronald McNicoll,
    Walter Ramsay McNicoll 1877-1947, page 57

Chapter Two

Una's wearing of purple and green brooch, as told to author by Joan
    Crommelin, February 2001

'I got in by the skin of my teeth', Cumberland letters, held by the
    Australian War Memorial

'Thousands of Union Jacks fluttered', told by L. L. Robson, *The First
    A.I.F. A Study of Its Recruitment 1914–1918*, page 35

Enlistment figures from E. Scott, *Official History of Australia in the
    War of 1914–18*, Vol XI, Appendix III

Renditions of 'Rule Britannia', L. L. Robson, page 24

'Spy-mania', E. Scott

'Hundreds of thousands of Australians', Geoffrey Blainey, *Eye On Australia*, page 223

Australia 'didn't know what it was like', Les Carlyon, *Gallipoli*, page 117

Australians wearing identity discs to their eyes, told in John Robertson, *Anzac and Empire*, page 37

Chapter Three

Simpson's hoping to go to England, Private John Simpson (Kirkpatrick) letters, AWM

'In your tucker, in your ears', quoted in Bill Gammage, page 44

New words such as *imshee yalla*, told in Charles Bean, page 218

'They are the funniest people on earth', Cumberland letters, AWM

Sentry joke, told in John Robertson, page 43

'Rather naughty', quoted in John Robertson, page 40

'Australians are notorious characters', quoted in John Robertson, page 41

Kitchener's 'spectacles flashed', Ian Hamilton, *Gallipoli Diary, Vol I*, page 8

'All through our history such attacks', quoted in Cecil Aspinall-Oglander, *Military Operations: Gallipoli, Vol I*, page 101

Chapter Four

'The boys are talking like a lot of school kids', quoted in Bill Gammage, page 49

Darnell forgetting to draw his revolver, quoted in Peter Bowers, *Anzacs*, page 17

'Black clouds', quoted in Robert Rhodes James, page 114

'How we prayed', quoted in Robert Rhodes James, page 115

'The way our chaps', Private Arthur Blackburn letters, AWM

'It was a case of a quick search', quoted in Ronald McNicoll, page 61

'We rejoiced as we gripped our rifles', quoted in Gammage, page 56

Evacuation figures given in Charles Bean, *Vol II*

'I know it's right and proper', quoted in Gammage page 59

Chapter Five

'I must remind all of you', quoted in Robert Rhodes James,
    page 166

'Absolute minimum', quoted in A. G. Butler, *Official History of the
    Australian Army Medical Services*, page 120

'Only one 18-pounder landed by 6 pm', Les Carlyon, page 166

'He was so short of ammunition', told in Charles Bean, page 435

'Found myself in the semi-darkness', Ellis Ashmead-Bartlett, *The
    Uncensored Dardanelles*, page 48

'I know my representation is most serious', Ian Hamilton, page 143

'You have got through the difficult business', Ian Hamilton,
    page 144

'Una I don't know how Joe is at present', Cumberland letters, AWM

'Poor Joe is gone' Cumberland letters, AWM

'Bearded, ragged at knees', Bean, *Vol I*, page 535

'For my own part I had no overcoat', Ivor Margetts letters, AWM

Chapter Six

'Pock-marked with caves', Ian Hamilton, page 178

'They are like masterless men', quoted in Jock Phillips, Nicholas
    Boyack and E. P. Malone, *The Great Adventure*, page 44

'F . . . ing old bastard Neptune', quoted in Robert Rhodes James,
    page 178

'We received the same old shells today', *The Gallipoli Diary of
    Sergeant Lawrence*, edited by Ronald East, page 34

'Yet everything works as smoothly as on a peace parade', *War Letters
    of General Monash*, edited by Tony Macdougall, page 55

'We are all of us certain', Tony Macdougall, page 48

'Very valuable in demonstrating', quoted in Christopher Pugsley,
Gallipoli: The New Zealand Story, page 183

'Casualties?' quoted in Compton Mackenzie, *Gallipoli Memories*,
page 152

'Are you hit?' quoted in Ronald McNicoll, page 68

'The machine guns bellowed and poured on them sheets of flame',
quoted in Ronald McNicoll, page 69

'Many men had been hit before reaching the Tommies' Trench',
Charles Bean, *Official History of Australia in the War of 1914-18*,
Vol II, page 39

'Hullo, old man; you up here?' quoted in Charles Bean, *Gallipoli
Mission*, page 294

'Dull, stupid, cruel bungling', quoted in *Gallipoli Correspondent*,
edited by Kevin Fewster, page 99

Chapter Seven

'Have they?' quote from Compton Mackenzie, page 81

Detail on Simpson and his donkeys taken from John Robertson,
page 93

Detail of Annie's brooch, *Simpson and the Donkey*, Peter Cochrane,
page 30

'We would like a few lines', Simpson letters, AWM

Chapter Eight

Estimation of rounds fired, given in John Robertson, page 94

'We got up to all sorts of dodges', quoted in John Robertson, page 94

'I managed to get the beggars, sir', quoted in Charles Bean, *Vol II*,
page 150

'Hey, have any of you muckers', quoted in Compton Mackenzie,
page 79

'Looking down I saw squelching up from the ground', Compton
    Mackenzie, page 83

'Not wounded but killed, their heads doubled under them', Aubrey
    Herbert, *Mons, Anzac and Kut*, page 139

Chapter Nine

'Men lived through more in five minutes on that crest',
    Ian Hamilton, page 258

'Now we have given them a sporting chance', quoted in Phillip
    Schuler, *Australia in Arms*, page 196

'They have a peculiar smell', *The Gallipoli Diary of Sergeant Lawrence*,
    page 28

'Good God, I never want to see', *The Gallipoli Diary of Sergeant
    Lawrence*, page 26

'Just as we were crossing Shrapnel Gully', Ion Idriess, *The Desert
    Column*, page 376

'Like a lot of sparrows on a perch', *The Gallipoli Diary of Sergeant
    Lawrence*, page 28

'Oh, Hell', Phillip Schuler, page 171

'There were friends going every day', quoted in Maurice Shadbolt,
    Voices of Gallipoli, page 90

'The awful look on a man's face after he has been bayoneted',
    A. B. Facey, *A Fortunate Life*, page 258

'A sort of love and trust in one another developed', A. B. Facey,
    page 275

'Roy was in pieces when they found him', A. B. Facey, page 267

'It wasn't so bad', A. B. Facey, page 261

'Blue-black mixture', Joe Murray, *Gallipoli As I Saw It*, page 76

'The flies are simply unbearable', Cecil McAnulty diary, AWM

Food and water rations given in Charles Bean, Vols I and II.

'The happiest man alive', H. R. McLarty letters, AWM

'The sea is nearly always', *The Gallipoli Diary of Sergeant Lawrence*,
    page 35

'It's absolutely piteous to see', *The Gallipoli Diary of Sergeant
    Lawrence*, page 46

Indians' camp, Phillip Schuler, page 181

'Anyhow, I don't think that they could do it', *The Gallipoli Diary of
    Sergeant Lawrence*, p58

Chapter Ten

'Going off his head', quoted in Ross McMullen, *Pompey Elliot*,
    page 130

'Nothing; not a nosebag nor a bicycle', Ian Hamilton, *Vol II*, page 51

Chapter Eleven

'This is hell waiting here', Cecil McAnulty diary, AWM

'The fire was simply hellish', quoted in Bill Gammage, page 69

'We was like a mob of ferrets', quoted in Kit Denton, *Gallipoli:
    One Long Grave*, page 87

Deaths from friendly fire at Lone Pine, asserted by Robert Rhodes
    James, page 265

'Many were killed within a few minutes', Charles Bean, *Vol II*,
    page 507

Avoiding treading on the faces of the dead, quoted in Bean, *Vol II*,
    page 532

'We had no time to think of our wounded', J. K. Gammage diary,
    AWM

'For God's sake send bombs', quoted in Bean, *Vol II*, page 533

'I remember dropping down', Cecil McAnulty diary, AWM

'Yet all one gave him was simply a casual glance', *The Gallipoli Diary
    of Sergeant Lawrence*, page 68

'One mass of dead bodies', *The Gallipoli Diary of Sergeant Lawrence*,
   pp 68–69

'In the trench I counted', Ivor Margetts letters, AWM

'Of all the bastards of places in the world', Ion Idriess, page 396

Details of William Dunstan's life from Keith Dunstan, the *Bulletin*,
   30 April 1996

Details of VC winners given in Stephen Snelling, *VCs of The First
   World War*, pages 165 and 177

'You can understand Una, that losing Joe has broken me up a bit',
   Cumberland letters, AWM

Details of Lone Pine found in *The Gallipolian*, winter 2001–01, and
   Legacy notes

'The trench was literally floored with dead', Charles Bean, *Vol II*,
   page 551

Chapter Twelve

'He made me a nice cover', quoted in the *Genealogist*,
   September 1996

Details of Victorians taken prisoner given in *The Lost Anzacs*, Greg
   Kerr, page 98; and in *The History of the Fourteenth Battalion AIF*,
   Wanliss Newton

'My men are not going to commit suicide', quoted in Maurice
   Shadbolt, page 62

'It's only when your tongue actually rattles', quoted in Shadbolt,
   page 93

'Blood was flying about like spray', quoted in Harry Davies, *Allanson
   of the 6th*, page 51

Chapter Thirteen

'One continuous roaring tempest', quoted in Peter Burness, *The Nek*,
   page 101

'As though their limbs had become string', Charles Bean, *Vol II*,
page 614

'Million ton hammer', Cliff Pinnock letters, AWM

'The only thing I could see worth shooting', McGarvie family letters

'There was no chance whatever', Cliff Pinnock letters, AWM

'They just mowed them down', McGarvie family letters

'I got within about six yards', quoted in Burness, page 108

Details of Trooper White's charge given in Burness, page 105

'Push on', and 'I am sorry lads', quoted in Burness, page 113

'A bob in and the winner shouts', quoted in Burness, page 117

'At first here and there a man raised his arm to the sky', Charles
Bean, *Vol II*, page 633

'Godley's abattoir', quoted in Christopher Pugsley, page 284

'Yes, it was heroic', quoted in Burness, page 126

Chapter Fourteen

'On the hills we are the eyebrows', Aubrey Herbert, page 192

'Birdie and Godley are at work upon a scheme', Ian Hamilton,
Vol II, page 90

'Inclined to be aggressive', quoted in Robert Rhodes James,
page 304

'Another mismanaged soldier', Ellis Ashmead-Bartlett, page 189

'Weak as cats', quoted in Robert Rhodes James, page 303

'Writhing bodies trying to get away', quoted in *The Genealogist*,
September 1996

Details of Myles O'Reilly from O'Reilly family letters

'We were in such a cramped position', James Grieve letter, AWM

'The whole was a rotten, badly organised show', quoted in
Peter Pedersen, *Monash as Military Commander*, page 119

Chapter Fifteen

'I do not pretend to understand the situation', quoted in the *Argus*,
30 October 1915

Chapter Sixteen

'You'd say it was childish', *The Gallipoli Diary of Sergeant Lawrence*,
page 120

'It is very quiet where we are', James Martin letters, AWM

'There was one Turk who tried to give himself up,' James Martin
letters, AWM

'Blood has drained out of bodies', Mehmed Fasih, *Lone Pine (Bloody
Ridge) Diary of Lieutenant Mehmed Fasih*, page 32

'I can't stand it any more', Fasih, pages 60-61

'Will I ever have a child who will call me "Daddy"?', Fasih,
page 123

Chapter Seventeen

'If it were true, God', *The Gallipoli Diary of Sergeant Lawrence*,
page 126

'Stupendous and paralysing', *War Letters of General Monash*, page 88

'Better to struggle and die fighting', *The Gallipoli Diary of Sergeant
Lawrence*, page 130

'I hope they won't hear us marching back', quoted in Cecil
Aspinall-Oglander, *Vol II*, page 453

'The last day was simply awful', Cliff Pinnock letters, AWM

'My God, I would have given anything in the world', Cliff Pinnock
letters, AWM

'It's a pity not to use them', quoted in W. J. Harvey, *The Red and
White Diamond: Official History of the 24th Battalion AIF*, page 56

'It was a most brilliant conception', *War Letters of General Monash*,
page 98

Chapter Eighteen

'Dear little wife and kiddie', quoted in Peter Burness, page 75

'I have never recovered from my 1914–18 experiences', quoted in Stephen Snelling, page 228

'I suppose that on some day, on some high plateau', *War Letters of General Monash*, page 62

Acknowledgments

There has been so much documented on Gallipoli that one could spend many years researching a book on the campaign. Half the battle, when tackling the subject – and working to a deadline – is to figure out what's important and what's not. Many people deserve thanks for steering me in the right direction.

The battlegrounds themselves make little sense without expert guidance. I thank Kenan Celik, who patiently guided me over Anzac and Suvla. Ashley Ekins and Ian Kelly, from the Australian War Memorial, allowed me to tag along with their Gallipoli tour in 2000. Peter Burness allowed me to quote from his book, *The Nek*, as did Christopher Pugsley from *Gallipoli: The New Zealand Story*; Bill Gammage from *The Broken Years*; Ross McMullin from *Pompey Elliott*; and Greg Kerr, from *Lost Anzacs*.

Like all who research Gallipoli, I found the two volumes of Charles Bean's *Official History of Australia in the War of 1914–18* to be invaluable. Sir Ian Hamilton's *Gallipoli Diary* shed much light on the problems of the campaign.

My thanks go to the numerous people who allowed me use of letters and diaries: Dr Margaret Heese, daughter of Sergeant Cyril Lawrence; Betty Durre, granddaughter of Sir John Monash; Judy Malone, widow of E. P. Malone

(Colonel Malone's grandson); Diana Cousens, granddaughter of Brigadier Walter Cass; Christine Gascoyne and David Collyer, grandchildren of Private David McGarvie; Robin Ashwin, nephew of Lance Corporal Phil Robin; Tom O'Reilly, son of Private Myles O'Reilly; Joan Crommelin, niece of privates Joe and Oliver Cumberland; Jack Harris, nephew of Private James Martin; Bill Gammage, great-nephew of Private John Gammage; Phil Brotchie, grandson of Private 'Dad' Brotchie; Major Harry Davies, nephew of Colonel Allanson; Keith Dunstan, son of Corporal William Dunstan; and Andrew Denton, son of Kit Denton.

Material has been quoted from the following texts: *Walter Ramsay McNicoll 1877–1947*, reproduced with permission of the trustees of the estate of Ronald Ramsay McNicoll; 'A Battle for a Mammoth Prize', by Geoffrey Blainey; *A Fortunate Life*, A. B. Facey, 1981, reproduced with permission of Penguin Books Australia Ltd; *Gallipoli*, Robert James Rhodes, Pimlico, 1999, used by permission of The Random House Group, *Gallipoli Memories*, Compton Mackenzie, Cassell, 1929, reproduced with permission of the Society of Authors as the literary representative of the estate of Compton Mackenzie; *Monash as Military Commander*, Peter Pedersen, 1992, reproduced with permission of Melbourne University Publishing; *Guns and Brooches*, Jan Bassett, 1992, reproduced with permission of Oxford University Press; *Voices of Gallipoli*, Maurice Shadbolt, 2001, reproduced with permission of David Ling Publishing;

Anzacs, Peter Bowers, 1999, reproduced with permission of Australia Post; *Gallipoli Correspondent*, Kevin Fewster, 1983, reproduced with permission of Allen and Unwin.

A book demands patience, mostly from those around the author. I thank my editor, Sandy Webster, for her sense of humour. I thank my agent, Deborah Callaghan, for her guidance in uncertain times. I thank my friends and family for so graciously accepting my self-imposed exile in the final stages of writing this book.

Any errors of fact are mine.

Photographic Credits

Front Cover

Photograph of the 7th Battalion machine-gun section courtesy of the Australian War Memorial AWM J05577

Inside Front Cover

Photograph of Lieutenant Price with an unexploded Turkish shell courtesy of the Australian War Memorial AWM C02052.

Inside Back Cover

Photograph of Private David McGarvie courtesy of David Collyer and Christine Gascoyne.

Picture Inserts

The publisher gratefully acknowledges permission from the Australian War Museum to reproduce a number of images, as credited.

Photographs of Joe and Oliver Cumberland courtesy of Joan Crommelin.

Photograph of Trooper Alfred Cameron Jnr courtesy of South Australian Museum Archives.

Photograph of Phil and Nellie Robin and Arthur Blackburn courtesy of Robin Ashwin.

The author would like to thank Mr E. B. LeCutaeur and Mrs A. M. Carroll for permission to use the illustration on page 96.

Index